TH...OR

BY
STEPHANIE HOWARD

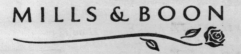

MILLS & BOON

MILLS & BOON LIMITED
ETON HOUSE, 18-24 PARADISE ROAD
RICHMOND, SURREY TW9 1SR

All the characters in this book have no existence outside the imagination of the Author, and have no relation whatsoever to anyone bearing the same name or names. They are not even distantly inspired by any individual known or unknown to the Author, and all the incidents are pure invention.

*MILLS & BOON and the Rose Device
are trademarks of the publisher.*

*First published in Great Britain 1994
by Mills & Boon Limited*

© Stephanie Howard 1994

*Australian copyright 1994   Philippine copyright 1994
This edition 1994*

ISBN 0 263 78580 7

*Set in Times Roman 11 on 12 pt.
01-9408-47703 C*

Made and printed in Great Britain

CHAPTER ONE

THIS was one of Charlotte's favourite times of day.

She stepped out of the drawing-room into the conservatory that was still deliciously warm from the heat of the day, and crossed to the cane table where her painting things lay. She loved having the big house all to herself. Its beautiful, familiar rooms felt companionable and cosy, and its silence was good for her concentration.

Charlotte smiled contentedly as she seated herself at the table and arranged her brushes and pots of paint. 'Are you sure you're not lonely up in the manor house on your own?' Ellen had asked her just that very evening.

And Charlotte had shaken her blonde head and answered, 'No, it's perfect. I couldn't be happier with the arrangement.'

'Well, if you get lonely, remember we're just at the end of the driveway. Drop in and see us any time you like,' Ellen had insisted in her kindly way.

And little Lucas had added, making them both laugh, 'If you get scared in the night, you can come and sleep in my bed.'

Charlotte had bent and kissed the head of Ellen's bright little three-and-a-half-year-old. 'That's very kind of you,' she'd told him. 'But do you think there'd be enough room for me *and* Bertie Rabbit?'

'Oh, yes,' the child had assured her earnestly. 'Bertie Rabbit and me don't take up much room.'

Seated now at the cane table in the huge conservatory that overlooked the rambling grounds of Penforth Manor, set in the heart of leafy Suffolk, Charlotte reached for the sketches she'd been working on last night and cast a critically appraising eye over them.

They weren't bad, she decided, and Lucas had liked them. In fact, he'd jumped up and down with approval! 'It's Bertie Rabbit!' he'd squealed. 'You've drawn Bertie Rabbit!' But the real test would come when she sent them off to the editor of the London publishing house she'd been in touch with. Then she would know if she'd got herself a new career!

For a moment she let her gaze drift out into the garden, a look of nervous excitement on her pretty grey-eyed face with its tip-tilted nose and soft rosebud mouth. She'd been dreaming of it for years and now she was finally on the verge of becoming a published writer and illustrator of children's books.

Then with a shake of her head Charlotte jolted herself back to reality. 'You don't make dreams come true by gazing into space,' she chided herself. 'You make them come true by dedication and hard work!'

Reaching for a paintbrush, she pushed back the sleeves of her gingham shirt. Don't waste time, she told herself. This arrangement at the mansion isn't going to last forever. You won't always have so much free time and such a perfect place to work. So make the most of every minute!

It was two hours later, as she was carefully colouring in one of her sketches, that Charlotte suddenly thought she heard a noise.

She sat up straight, cocked her head and listened, but all she could hear from the big house was silence. I'm imagining things, she decided, and carried on working.

But a couple of minutes later she heard something again, something that definitely wasn't her imagination, and it seemed to be coming from one of the rooms behind her. She felt a clench of apprehension, suddenly very conscious that she was all alone in the big empty house, and that while she'd been working night had fallen, cloaking the surrounding grounds in darkness. Suddenly her grip on her paintbrush had tightened.

And there was that noise again. She held her breath and listened. It was like a floorboard creaking or a door hinge squeaking. Suddenly she was quite certain. There was someone else in the house.

A rush of panic went through her. It must be an intruder. If it were Ellen or her husband Ted, they'd have made themselves known. She swallowed and turned to stare at the open door behind her that led from the conservatory back into the drawing-room. The only lights she'd switched on were the lights in the conservatory. Only if the intruder saw those would he know she was here.

She rose stiffly from her seat, dry-mouthed, swallowing hard. If she closed the door and switched off the lights, then just stayed where she was and didn't make a sound, perhaps the intruder would just finish what he'd come for and leave. It wasn't the most heroic strategy in the world, but there might be more than one intruder and they might be armed.

Charlotte's heart was hammering as she crept towards the door, reaching for the light switch on the wall beside it. Then, with a gasp of relief, she had switched the lights off and was grabbing for the door-handle to push the door shut.

But she was too late. Already, the door was being pushed wider and she let out a cry of uncontrolled panic as, in the inky blackness that suddenly surrounded her, a male figure came bursting through the doorway, colliding straight into her and grabbing her by the arm.

Charlotte thought she might faint. She felt her blood drain away. But then, instinctively, she struggled with all her strength.

'Let me go! I've already called the police! They'll be here any minute,' she squeaked defensively, rather impressed at her powers of invention. After all, there wasn't even a phone in the conservatory!

In spite of her struggles and protests, however, the intruder was still holding firmly on to her, his fingers a band of steel around her arm.

'I think I'm the one who should be calling the police.' As he spoke, his grip around her arm seemed to tighten. 'Who the devil are you? And what are you doing here?'

'What am *I* doing here?'

As her eyes adjusted to the darkness, slightly softened by the moonlight that glanced through the glass panes of the conservatory, Charlotte could make out a few basic details about her assailant.

He was very tall—frighteningly tall from where she stood!—mid-thirties, broad-shouldered and muscularly built. But there was something odd. He didn't look like an intruder. He wasn't wearing a mask or a stocking over his face, and he wore nothing on his head to hide the thick dark hair that glistened like polished ebony in the moonlight. In fact, he'd made no attempt whatsoever to disguise himself. He was wearing a perfectly regular dark suit.

'That's what I asked you. What are *you* doing here?'

As he repeated his question, he had half turned away from her to quickly flick on the light switch behind him. And as the conservatory was suddenly flooded with light, Charlotte felt a rush of relief go through her, instantly, if belatedly, recognising who he was.

'You're Jett Ashton!' She'd thought he was in New York! And though he was not someone she would normally be overjoyed to see, she was now, wholeheartedly and without reservation!

As she looked into his face, she sagged with relief, her legs, which had been like ramrods, slackening gratefully beneath her. 'Thank heavens for that,' she breathed. 'I thought you were an intruder.'

'No, I'm afraid *you*'re the intruder.' Jett regarded her harshly, not even a ghost of answering recognition in his expression. And his grip around her arm was as tight as ever as he demanded, glaring at her, 'What are you doing in my house?'

'But surely you know who I am and what I'm doing here!' Charlotte frowned into his face, feeling a spark of uneasiness. 'Ted told you! He told you weeks ago! Had you forgotten that I was staying here?'

'Ted told me nothing.' Jett bit the words at her impatiently. Then he gave her a sharp shake. 'Explain yourself,' he demanded.

Charlotte was aware of a sinking feeling inside her. Knowing what she did of Jett Ashton's character, it had occurred to her on more than one occasion that this arrangement at the manor house was almost too good to be true. And now, as she looked into his harsh dark face, all her worst fears seemed about to be confirmed.

It was very clear that the new owner of Penforth Manor didn't want her staying in his house.

'You at least know who I am, surely?' she began uneasily. 'I know we only met once before, and that was only for a couple of minutes. But you do recognise me, don't you? I was your uncle Oscar's nurse in the months before he died.'

'Uncle Oscar's nurse?' Jett's eyes narrowed as he looked at her. And it really was a little insulting that there wasn't even the faintest spark of recognition there. Especially, Charlotte thought, considering the fact that she had recognised him instantly!

But then how could she not have? she reflected wryly. There were few men around who looked like Jett Ashton!

For he was, without the faintest shadow of doubt, the most striking-looking man she had ever encountered. Tall, magnificently built, with a head of coal-black hair and eyes that were bluer than any mortal had a right to, he was a man who, once seen, was never likely to be forgotten. And it wasn't just his looks. It was his powerful aura. One encounter with him and he was burned in one's memory forever.

He was continuing to frown down at her. 'So, you're Charlotte Channing?'

The blue eyes swept over her for a moment, taking in the shoulder-length golden-blonde hair that was secured in a clasp at the nape of her neck, moving unhurriedly over the red gingham blouse that moulded the generously full curves of her breasts, then to the slender feminine waist and softly flaring hips, currently accentuated by the baggy jeans she was wearing.

'I'm afraid I didn't recognise you without your uniform,' he observed, smiling.

'But you ought to have known it was me, anyway.' A flush had risen to Charlotte's throat at the coolly appraising way he had just examined her, rather like the way he had examined her before on that one brief meeting just over nine months ago.

She'd thought then as she'd met the impudent arrogance in his face that he was obviously every bit as bad as he'd been painted—for all the stories she'd heard about him were far from flattering. And as she looked at him now she was thinking the same thing.

'As I said already,' she added a little tightly, 'Ted told you I was going to be staying here at the manor.'

He had released his hold on her very slightly. 'And as I said already, Ted told me no such thing.' Jett regarded her down the length of his arrogant, shapely nose. 'What on earth possessed you to think for one moment that I would enter into such an arrangement with Ted?'

'Ellen told me you had.'

'Then I'm afraid she misled you. I am very definitely not in the habit of entering into any kind of agreement with her husband.'

He had no need to elaborate. His sharp tone said it all. And, anyway, Charlotte was already aware of the bad blood that existed between Jett Ashton and his cousin Ted, husband of the sweet-natured Ellen. She knew also that at the root of it lay Jett Ashton's hard heart and that, nine months ago, it had reduced poor Ellen to floods of tears.

Without any hesitation she knew whose side she was on—and, anyway, she didn't believe his current denials!

'I'm sure Ted must have told you. Perhaps it slipped your mind?' Her grey eyes were sceptical as she offered this explanation. More likely, she was thinking, he had simply changed his mind!

Jett met her frank gaze with the hint of a smile. Charlotte sensed he knew more or less what she was thinking, and that he didn't give a damn.

But then, according to the legend, Jett gave a damn about nothing. And the legend, he was fast proving to her, was one hundred per cent right!

He had released his hold on her and was leaning against the door-frame, his shoulders very broad beneath the expensively tailored jacket, his hands thrust contemptuously into his trouser pockets.

'Very well, then. Let us assume that I suffer from a defective memory...'

His eyes glanced across her face, distracting Charlotte for a moment. Those eyes of his were quite remarkable, she was thinking. Brighter and bluer than any sapphires. Then she forced her attention back to what he was saying, as he continued,

'Perhaps you would grant me the favour of reminding me of the details of this agreement that I entered into with my cousin?'

'My pleasure.' Charlotte gratefully took a step back away from him, feeling her arm tingle warmly where he had gripped her. Pig! she was thinking. How dare he manhandle me like that!

She folded her arms across her chest and proceeded to tell him what she was sure he was already aware of.

'The arrangement is this . . . I'm to be allowed to stay on in my old room—the room that was mine while I was nursing your uncle Oscar—for as long as I'm looking after Lucas for Ellen and Ted. As you know, they have no spare room in their house—and there are dozens of spare rooms here,' she couldn't resist adding.

Jett ignored that remark. Instead, he narrowed his blue eyes at her. 'You said you're looking after Lucas. I wasn't aware that he was ill?'

That had sounded almost as though he cared about the child, which Charlotte knew perfectly well he didn't. Jett was barely acquainted with his cousin's little son. But, all the same, it was a nice touch, she couldn't help thinking.

'Lucas isn't ill,' she reassured him. 'But he needs someone to look after him while Ted and Ellen are out at work. Ellen's had to go back to work, you see. They're finding it hard to make ends meet.'

'Spare me the sob story,' Jett interrupted harshly. 'Just get on with your explanations.'

Charlotte took a deep breath, her eyes shooting daggers. He didn't give a damn about his poor cousin's financial problems, either.

'That's it, really,' she told him. 'They've hired me to look after Lucas until they can find a suitable child-minder. Ted contacted you in New York to check that it would be OK for me to stay on in my old room here while I'm working for them. And you, so Ellen told me, said it would be.'

'That was most generous of me.' Jett straightened suddenly and paused to look down at her for a moment. Then, detaching his gaze, he stepped past her into the conservatory, glancing round at the greenery as he added, 'I'm surprised they can afford you if they're so hard up. I seem to remember my uncle mentioning that you don't exactly come cheap.'

'I don't, as a rule.' Charlotte followed him with her eyes as he came to a halt beside a flowering blue orchid. 'When I'm hired as a private nurse I charge private nursing rates—or, at least, the agency I work for does. But since I'm not doing any nursing, just a bit of child-minding, I'm charging Ellen and Ted a considerably lower rate.'

Jett turned briefly to glance at her. 'How very self-sacrificing. Aren't there any private nursing jobs around these days?'

'There are always plenty of private nursing jobs.'

'Then why are you working for Ted and Ellen?'

'I'm doing them a favour. Is that so strange? And, anyway, I enjoy looking after Lucas.'

Jett flicked her a glance, then turned to the flowering orchid and raised one of the bright blue blooms to his nose. 'I suppose looking after a three-year-old child,' he observed, 'makes a pleasant change from looking after a cantankerous old man?'

'What an unkind remark.'

'You think so, do you?'

'He was your uncle. And, though I know he could sometimes be difficult, he was very old and he was dying.'

Jett smiled and shook his head. 'How very loyal you are. Though I can assure you your loyalty is gravely misplaced. My uncle Oscar was cantankerous by nature long before he was either old or dying.'

Is that why you never visited him? Charlotte resisted the temptation to say it. Coming from someone who was staying in his house, such a remark would be neither diplomatic nor polite!

'In fact, I'm surprised you put up with him for as long as you did.' Jett's long tanned fingers hovered over the orchid. 'How long were you with him? It must have been nearly a year.'

'It was eleven months. And he wasn't hard to put up with. Your uncle was no more difficult than most old people.'

Which was more or less true, Charlotte reflected to herself, though she had to admit he had definitely had his moments!

'Having Ellen and Ted around helped,' she added. 'They were always there to give me a bit of moral support.'

'Ah, yes, Ellen and Ted.' Jett smiled a cynical smile. 'I imagine they were glued to the old boy's bedside.'

'They visited him a lot.'

'Every day, I've no doubt.'

'Yes, every day. And sometimes more than once.'

'I'm surprised they didn't move in.' Jett's tone was cutting. Then he paused. 'But, of course, they didn't need to move in. These days they live just a stone's throw away.' Again he smiled that darkly cynical smile. 'My, wasn't it good of them to move into the Coach House, right here on the estate?'

Charlotte guessed what he was suggesting in his darkly cynical way. He was suggesting that Ted and Ellen had had some ulterior motive for moving into the Coach House that stood at the end of the manor house driveway—like the hope of benefiting from Uncle Oscar's will. But Jett was way off the mark and Charlotte strongly disapproved of his attempt deliberately to twist the facts.

In a cool tone she reminded him, 'It was your uncle Oscar who did them a favour. Three years ago, when Ted's company collapsed and he and Ellen lost their house in London, he very kindly offered them the Coach House, rent free. They've told me often they couldn't have survived without that.'

'I'm sure they couldn't have.' Jett smiled a flippant smile. It was clear he couldn't have cared less if they'd wound up in the gutter.

Spurred by his callousness, Charlotte continued with what she'd been telling him.

'In case you weren't aware of it, Ted and Ellen have always known that your uncle planned to leave everything to you. They told me they knew. They told me that months ago.'

She paused and fixed him with a censorious grey eye that told him she personally disagreed with the old man's judgement, even if Jett was the old man's oldest surviving male relative.

'So, you see,' she added, returning to her point, 'what Ted and Ellen did for your uncle they did out of love and gratitude, not in the hope of gain.'

'Regular saints, eh?'

'Not saints. Just good people.'

'Then no doubt they will have their reward in heaven.'

As he said it, Jett smiled and plucked the blue orchid. Then he added, as with a satisfied nod of his head he slipped the bloom into the lapel buttonhole of his jacket,

'Personally, I prefer to have mine in this world.'

Charlotte watched him for a moment from beneath her lashes. With every syllable he uttered he was living up to his reputation.

'He's a tough, totally ruthless and brilliant businessman,' Ted had told her on many occasions. 'He runs a multi-national company that's literally worth billions. But making money, alas, is all Jett cares about. He doesn't have a single compassionate bone in his body.

And Charlotte was starting to see that every word of that was true.

Jett was flicking her a glance now, smiling a cool, sardonic smile. 'You know, I've always found it rather surprising that Uncle Oscar made that generous offer of the Coach House. Generosity, as a rule, wasn't his strong point.'

'You knew him well, did you?'

She knew the opposite to be the case and her tone of voice was full of censure. Jett Ashton had never made any effort to know his uncle. He'd cared no more about the old man than he did about anyone else.

'I knew all I needed to know.' Jett was unperturbed by her sharpness. He smiled again. 'I was brought up in the States. On the other side of the Atlantic,' he added, just in case she needed a geography lesson. 'And that's where I'm based now, in case you didn't know. Quite a few miles from Penforth Manor.'

Charlotte already knew about his American background, but she also knew it was a pretty poor excuse. She pointed out to him, 'But these days, surely, your business brings you to London fairly often?'

Ted had told her he came over virtually every other month, yet, though it was just over an hour's drive from the centre of London to Penforth Manor, his visits to see his uncle had been brief and infrequent.

'Yes, I visit London quite a lot.'

At least he didn't deny it. But then he was not the type of man who would deny things, Charlotte sensed. He'd just look you in the eye and not give a damn what you thought.

He continued, 'However, I usually have a pretty full programme when I'm here. Unlike Ted and Ellen, I couldn't just drop everything in order to be at my uncle's bedside.' The blue eyes narrowed. 'I'm afraid I had better things to do.'

Charlotte felt herself flinch a little at his hardness. Yes, every single word of what Ted had said was true!

She looked into the blue eyes. 'So what brings you here now? Don't you have better things to do?'

Again he simply smiled at the sharpness in her tone. You had to hand it to him—his poise was unshakeable.

He said, 'I suppose I do, but in the interests of duty I've decided to put aside a couple of weeks so I can devote myself to the needs of Penforth Manor.'

'You mean you'll be staying for two weeks?'

'That's right.'

'I see.'

Charlotte felt her heart sink to the soles of her shoes. That was bad news for her. She'd obviously have to move out now. And it was bad news for Ellen and Ted as well. Ellen had told her Jett's presence always meant trouble. And, last time he was here, Charlotte had seen with her own eyes just how true that happened to be.

'I'm afraid Ted's reign of influence in the affairs of Penforth Manor is about to come to a rather abrupt end.' Jett smiled the smile of the cat that caught the mouse. 'What a pity all Ted's efforts, both business-wise and personal, were destined to come to nothing in the end.'

He really was unbearable. Charlotte narrowed her grey eyes at him. 'To talk of Ted's reign of influence, I'd say, was pushing it a bit. He helped your uncle with his accounts, but that was all.'

She took a deep breath. 'And I'll tell you something else. Ted doesn't care that his uncle left him nothing. I've certainly never heard either him or Ellen complain.'

There was admiration in her voice. They'd behaved with modesty and dignity. Two people less like Jett Ashton were impossible to imagine!

She couldn't resist adding, 'Perhaps, unlike you, they're happy to have their reward in heaven.'

'Perhaps they are.' Jett simply smiled cynically. 'They're obviously a great deal more patient than I am.'

Charlotte couldn't quite hold back an amused smile at that. 'Well, the powers that be are obviously aware of your lack of patience.' She cast an admiring eye round the huge conservatory. 'You certainly appear to be reaping your reward in this world.'

Jett stepped away from the flowering orchid and slipped his hands into his trouser pockets. He followed her gaze. 'This, you mean?'

'This, the house, all its fabulous contents ... The gardens, the grounds ... It's not a bad reward, I'd say.'

Charlotte smiled a little wryly as she said it. To a girl like her, raised in a council house in Derby, Penforth Manor and all its priceless contents amounted to wealth far beyond her wildest dreams. Not in all her twenty-four years had she seen anything like it until she'd stepped, wide-eyed, through the front door a year ago.

But she shook her head and shrugged now. 'But maybe to you it isn't much.'

She'd forgotten how rich he was. Fabulously rich, according to Ted and Ellen. In the private-jet and luxury-yacht bracket. Penforth Manor to him was probably just another house. Ellen had told her he already owned several around the world.

'Oh, it's a nice enough pile.' Jett looked back at her with amusement. 'I'm sure I'll manage to find some use for it.'

Then he paused and bent his head to the blue orchid in his lapel. 'You know, this is a very rare variety,' he told her, raising it to his nose and breathing in its fragrance. 'It's a scented orchid. Very special. Uncle Oscar travelled all the way to Malaysia to get it. He was quite passionate about orchids. But then I suppose you knew that?'

'Yes. He often told me about his orchids.'

'I'm sure he did. He told everyone about his orchids. And I can see his point...they're spectacular flowers...' He paused and seemed, very deliberately, to hold her gaze. 'Each to his own,' he added enigmatically. 'Personally, I tend to reserve my passions for other things.'

The way he'd looked at her had caused a flush to rise in Charlotte's cheeks. In his eyes, as exotically blue as the bloom in his buttonhole, for an instant she had seen something that had made her skin tingle. Taken by surprise, abruptly, she dropped her gaze.

She felt him smile. 'Which brings us to you.'

As she stared at the floor, a warning bell rang in Charlotte's head. Suddenly she was remembering something Ellen had told her.

'He's outrageous with women. A compulsive womaniser. He goes through girlfriends faster than other men go through socks.'

And if Charlotte wasn't mistaken, that was a line he'd just thrown her.

She raised her eyes sternly. I don't fall for lines, they were telling him. But as he smiled at her, to her horror, she felt that tingle again.

'Me?' she demanded, rather less aggressively than she'd intended.

'Yes, you.' With a casual shrug he half turned away from her, moving unhurriedly between the potted plants. 'I appear to have inherited you along with the house.' He glanced at her casually across his shoulder. 'An interesting, if unexpected, development.'

'I shall move out, of course.' She'd already decided to do so, anyway. 'I shall move out immediately,' she assured him.

'And where will you go?' He was glancing round him as he spoke. 'As you've already told me, Ted and Ellen have no spare room.'

'No, they don't, but I'm sure they'll find me some corner. I can always sleep on the sofa.'

There was no other solution, she was thinking. On the money that Ted and Ellen were paying her there was no way she could stretch to financing her own accommodation.

'What's this, then?'

He had come to a halt by the cane table where, before his arrival, Charlotte had been happily painting.

'Rabbits,' he continued. 'Rabbits with little hats on...' He turned to cast her an amused glance over his shoulder. 'I didn't know you were an artist.'

'I'm not!' Instantly defensive, Charlotte leapt forward as he picked up one of her paintings to study it more closely. 'They're nothing. I was just doodling.'

'They're rather good in a way. I'd say you have a talent.' Jett paused to deliver another amused glance. 'Not everyone can paint such charming little rabbits.'

Condescending pig! Charlotte glared at him fiercely and snatched the painting from his fingers. 'It's not dry,' she snapped, dropping it back on to the table. 'And, besides, these paintings happen to be private.'

'I see. So, that's *your* particular passion? Secretly painting rabbits with little hats on.'

'It's not a passion. It's just... It's just...nothing.'

Charlotte was aware that the sentence had started off quite firmly, only to peter out rather pathetically towards the end. Jett Ashton, she'd been thinking, was the very last person she was ever likely to dream of confiding in. These paintings and what they represented were too close to her heart. She would not allow them to become the butt of his jokes.

But as she'd been making her point, she'd suddenly become aware that in her anxiety to separate him from her paintings she had inadvertently placed herself between him and the table. And now she seemed to be trapped there and he was standing very close. No wonder she'd found it hard to finish the sentence!

Jett was looking down at her, unlike her, quite unperturbed by their sudden proximity. 'I don't think I much like the idea,' he was telling her, 'of you huddled on some sofa down at the Coach House.'

As he spoke, Charlotte could smell the perfume of the blue orchid. It was rich and exotic and it was going straight to her head.

Or, at least something was going straight to her head! All at once she felt quite weak and giddy.

Charlotte forced herself to say, 'That wouldn't be a problem. It wouldn't be the first time I've slept on a sofa.'

As she spoke, she tried to inch away and jarred her thigh against the table edge. Another move and the entire table, along with her paintpots and precious drawings, would be sent crashing chaotically to the ground!

So she froze where she was, bent back as far as she could manage, and held her breath as Jett shook his head.

'It sounds most unsatisfactory to me,' he said.

Charlotte swallowed. 'It doesn't to me. To me it sounds just fine.'

It was the black sweep of his lashes that made his eyes so extraordinary, Charlotte found herself thinking, as she continued to stand there. Suddenly, once again, her skin was tingling. With an effort she tore her gaze away.

'You could stay on here.'

'Here at the manor?' Something jolted inside her. Suddenly she was sweating. 'No, that's not possible. I can't afford to pay you rent.'

'I wasn't thinking of rent.'

'But I can't stay here for nothing... I mean not when you never wanted me here in the first place.'

'I might change my mind. I might decide I do want you.' Jett's gaze flitted over her, his lips curved in a smile. 'After all, it would be a shame to waste such an opportunity. You here and me here... all alone...'

He paused, then, to Charlotte's absolute horror, he slid one hand from his trouser pocket and reached up to tilt her chin with his fingers. And for

a moment she just stood there, frozen into im-
mobility by the firm cool touch of his fingers
against her skin, as he elaborated softly, his tone a
sensuous purr,

'I'm sure, if we tried, we could come to some
arrangement . . .'

CHAPTER TWO

'AN ARRANGEMENT? Exactly what kind of an arrangement?'

As Jett's fingers brushed her skin, making her tingle all over, Charlotte finally found the will-power to move away from him. As she spoke, her tone sharp, she had slid from her prison, suddenly not caring whether she knocked over the table! All that mattered was that she put some distance between them.

She narrowed her grey eyes at him. 'What are you suggesting?'

'Don't look so alarmed.' He cast an amused smile across at her and slipped his hand back in his pocket. 'I can assure you what I'm about to suggest is perfectly proper.'

Charlotte held his gaze. 'I'm glad to hear it. Just for a moment back there I wondered.'

'Then wonder no longer.'

His eyes danced over her, and Charlotte could tell from his amused look that he was thinking her foolish. What would a man like him want with a girl like her? She was not his type. He'd like his women flashy and glamorous. He wouldn't go in for jeans-clad nurses-cum-artists!

'What I was thinking was this...' Jett had stepped back away from her and was leaning casually against the trunk of a potted palm tree. 'In return for free bed and board at Penforth Manor, you can run the house for me.'

A servant! That was more like it. Someone to fetch and carry!

'I'm afraid that won't be possible. I'm with Lucas all day.' Besides, she added to herself, I'm damned if I'll run after you!

'Not all day, surely?' Jett was watching her closely. 'I understood that Lucas goes to nursery school in the morning?'

That surprised her. He knew more than she'd expected. 'Yes, he does,' she answered. 'I drop him off at nine and pick him up at noon. And then I'm with him for the rest of the day until five-thirty.'

'So, that leaves you with three spare hours in the morning, not to mention every evening and all weekend. Plenty of time to do what's needed.'

'I'm afraid it's impossible.'

Charlotte shook her head. She'd been about to add, 'I need all my spare time', but wisely she bit the words off in time. He would only want to know what she needed her spare time for and she had already decided to tell him nothing.

In fact, she needed her spare time to finish her paintings that were to accompany the stories she'd already written and that had more or less been accepted by a publisher in London. The sooner they were finished the sooner she could devote herself to setting herself up in her long-dreamed-of career.

And she'd promised she'd have the illustrations done by the end of June and now that was only two weeks away!

Keeping all that to herself, she looked at Jett Ashton. 'I'm sorry, I don't do that sort of work.'

'You do child-minding.'

'As a favour. I've already told you. And, besides, that arrangement is strictly temporary.'

'So would the one with me be. And it would save you moving to a bed on the sofa. And since I'll be busy you'd have the house to yourself most of the time.'

It was that promise that caused Charlotte finally to hesitate. If she moved to the cottage and a bed on the sofa, apart from the mornings, she would have little chance to get on with her painting. She just wouldn't have the privacy she needed.

A sense of helpless frustration went sweeping through her. She was so very close to achieving her goal. She couldn't bear to be thwarted now.

She fixed her grey eyes on Jett. 'How much free time would I have?'

'Ah, now we're getting somewhere.' He smiled with satisfaction. 'At last we have the basis for negotiation.' Then with a shrug of his broad shoulders, he straightened away from the palm tree. 'But it's late. Let's leave the negotiations till tomorrow. I'm a little tired. I've just flown in from New York.'

'I haven't agreed to anything. Don't take anything for granted.' Charlotte had the very strong suspicion that he already did. He probably couldn't imagine anyone not doing as he wished!

Jett smiled a knowing smile. 'We'll discuss it tomorrow. Over breakfast, if you like. After you've dropped off Lucas. I can't imagine I'll be up much before nine.'

'Very well, then.' Charlotte nodded a little tentatively. She had the feeling she was being sucked in against her will. In a firm tone she added, 'We'll discuss everything tomorrow morning and I'll come to a decision then.'

She would not, she told herself firmly, be sucked into anything!

'And now, bed. At least for me.' Jett was glancing at his watch. Then he paused before turning in the direction of the drawing-room and threw her a wink across his shoulder. 'I'm glad you've decided to be reasonable, after all.'

Don't count on it! Charlotte watched him disappear through the doorway, then turned with a sigh back to the table with her work things. At least he was right about one thing. It was time for bed.

She screwed the lids on to her paintpots and gathered up her brushes and loaded them all into her wooden painting case. Then as she snapped the fastenings shut she paused for a moment and gazed out through the conservatory to the moonlit garden.

It had all seemed so peaceful and so perfect until an hour ago. Now Jett had come crashing in and everything was ruined.

But then that was the effect his arrival always seemed to have, she reflected, casting her mind back to their first and only previous meeting . . .

It had been about nine months ago, one rainy autumn afternoon, and she'd been sitting with old Oscar upstairs in his room. The old man had been dozing and there'd really been no need for her to be there, but he'd been restless that morning and even more demanding than usual, so just in case he woke up and needed her she'd stayed.

She'd taken her notebook with her, the one where she wrote up all her stories—the Bertie Rabbit stories that went with the drawings—and she'd been bent over it, busily scribbling away, when suddenly behind her in the corridor a fearful commotion had broken out.

It was Ted's voice she'd recognised and he'd sounded upset. 'That's not true,' he was protesting. 'You have no right to say that!'

'I have every damned right!' another voice had cut in, impatient, angry and as cold as tempered steel. 'And now, if you don't mind, I'd be grateful if you'd get out of my way!'

Ted had evidently obliged, for an instant later clipped male footsteps were marching down the corridor. Charlotte had paused in her writing and glanced automatically at the door. A moment later it had flown open and Jett had stormed into the room.

He had looked straight at Charlotte. 'Leave us!' he had commanded. 'I want a word alone with my uncle.'

Charlotte had half risen in her seat, a little thrown by the dynamic power of him. And though she had never set eyes on him before, she had known without a doubt that this was Jett Ashton.

Feeling a strange twist inside her, she'd looked into his eyes, faintly startled by their vivid blueness. She had never seen eyes so blue before.

'But he's sleeping,' she'd responded with a nod at her patient. 'I really don't think he ought to be disturbed.'

'Then I won't disturb him. I'll wait until he wakes.' The blue eyes had fixed her, as cold as chips of ice. 'And now, if you don't mind, I've asked you to leave.'

'I'm leaving.' Charlotte had looked back at him, only one thought in her head. Ellen and Ted had told her he was a difficult man to deal with. But he wasn't just difficult. He was downright rude!

But Jett Ashton wasn't the first difficult or rude relative she'd had to deal with and she wasn't intimidated in the slightest.

On her way to the door she'd paused and looked at him, her expression composed, her grey eyes unblinking. 'Your uncle really shouldn't be upset. I would ask you to kindly bear that in mind.'

'Don't lecture me, young woman.' Jett's voice was a snarl. Narrowed blue eyes had sparked a warning back at her. Then he'd nodded towards the door. 'I won't ask you again.'

'I'll be back in half an hour.' She'd glanced at her watch. 'It'll be time for your uncle's injection then.' Then, taking her notebook with her, without another word, she'd left the room.

Out in the corridor, she'd paused to snatch a deep breath. In spite of her outward coolness, the encounter had shaken her. It had felt like the verbal equivalent of a mugging.

She'd sunk down into one of the chairs that were arranged along the corridor, noting that there was no sign of Ted any more. He'd probably gone off to pour himself a stiff drink!

It had been twenty-five minutes later when Ted and Ellen had reappeared and Charlotte had been busily scribbling in her notebook. She'd only become aware of them when Ellen had spoken.

'Is he still in there?' she'd asked in a nervous whisper.

Charlotte had nodded. 'And at least he's behaving himself, it seems. I've heard the occasional murmur, but no raised voices so far.'

'Poor Uncle Oscar. I wonder what Jett wants?' Ted had shaken his balding head, a frown creasing his brow. 'Whenever Jett appears it always means trouble.'

At that moment Charlotte had been about to nod sympathetically. But before she could do so the door had burst open again and she was aware of Ted and Ellen falling back with a gasp as Jett came sweeping out into the corridor.

It had all happened without a sound, she had reflected later. He had this ability to appear to come bursting through doors, simply thanks to the dynamic physical presence he possessed.

He'd glared at Charlotte, ignoring the other two. 'I thought you said my uncle was due to have an injection now.' He'd cast a sharp glance at the notebook in her hand. 'Perhaps when you've finished writing to your boyfriend, you wouldn't mind coming and giving it to him?'

Charlotte had flushed crimson. 'I wasn't writing to my boyfriend!'

'And you weren't looking after your patient, either—which is what my uncle is paying you to do.'

Her blush had grown even deeper if that were possible. 'How dare you accuse me of professional negligence? I wasn't looking after your uncle because he wasn't needing looking after. Take my word for it, when he does, I shall do my duty!'

'I'm afraid I can't take your word for it.' Jett's tone was steely. 'You told me half an hour ago he was due to have an injection now. I still see no sign of you coming to give it.'

'It's not necessary to give it right now.'

Charlotte had remembered what she'd said, but what she'd said had been a slight exaggeration. The injection still wasn't due for another fifteen minutes. She'd simply been hoping to encourage Jett to cut his visit short!

Well, that ploy had rebounded and now she was being made to look unprofessional. She'd straightened her shoulders beneath her blue and white uniform. 'What I said before wasn't strictly accurate. But don't worry, when it's time to give the injection I shall give it.'

Jett had not looked impressed. 'What's the name of your agency? I think it might be wise if I checked up on you.'

'Check all you like.' She'd given him the name without hesitation. 'You'll find there has never been a single complaint against me, ever.'

'If I do, I'll be satisfied. If I don't, you'll be fired.' Jett had smiled a grim smile. 'So, let's hope for your sake that you're right.' And with that he had stormed back into Uncle Oscar's room.

Later, once he had gone, Ellen had told her, 'Don't worry. I promise you nobody's going to fire you.'

'Thanks.'

To be truthful, Charlotte wasn't worried. She was a first-class nurse with an impeccable record. If she did find herself fired, it would be out of spite and nothing else.

But all the same she'd felt grateful for Ellen's kind words, particularly since the poor woman was still upset herself. For there'd been another row after Jett had left his uncle and gone downstairs.

Charlotte hadn't heard what it was about. All she'd heard were Jett and Ted's shouting voices. And when Ellen had come upstairs to bring her a cup of tea, Charlotte could see that she'd been crying.

She'd touched the woman's arm and smiled at her kindly. 'What a nasty man that Jett is. Everything you told me about him was right.'

'Oh, you don't know the half of it.' Ellen had shaken her head. Then she'd smiled a brave smile. 'But that's Ted's and my problem. Just you think no more about it. I promise you he can't touch you.'

Charlotte pursed her lips now thoughtfully as she stared out into the garden, her wooden painting case still held in her hands. That had been nine months ago and she'd never seen Jett again—he'd come over for his uncle's funeral at the beginning of last month, but that had been family only and she hadn't been present—and she'd rather been hoping that was the way things would remain.

She sighed. Vain hope. It looked as though Jett Ashton was about to become as big a thorn in her side as he was in everyone else's!

Careful not to smudge them, she gathered up her paintings and headed for the door that led back into the drawing-room. And, as she did so, she smiled wryly at the prospect of tomorrow's meeting. For somehow she couldn't envisage coming to an agreement with Jett Ashton—unless it was an agreement that each of them go their separate ways! And she had a feeling that was precisely what it would come to.

Locking the conservatory door behind her, she made her way through the drawing-room, then across the huge hall to the staircase and her room.

And it struck her, even more forcefully with every step she took, that the lovely old house suddenly no longer felt the same. Jett's dynamic disruptive presence seemed to crouch in every corner and fill the very air with an aura of lurking menace.

She shivered. She could definitely smell trouble on the way.

'Ah, there you are. Sit down and have some coffee.'

Jett was seated in the breakfast-room at the table in the bay window, dressed in light trousers and an open-neck shirt, with spread out before him an array of newspapers, one of which he'd been poring over when she stepped into the room.

He smiled at her. 'There's a pot somewhere, if you can find it.'

Charlotte smiled back at him with amusement. 'That might not be easy.' For the coffee-pot, along with everything else on the table, was buried under the mountain of newsprint!

Still, as she sat down opposite him, she managed to root it out, observing as she did so, 'I see you're hard at work already. Goodness me. Such dedication!'

Such ruthless single-mindedness, she was really thinking. For every newspaper, she had noticed, was turned to the business pages. Ted was right. All this man thought about was making money!

Though she hadn't intended him to, he had caught her faint edge of criticism. She could tell that was so as he smiled across at her, clearly as unmoved as ever by her censure.

'It's a lifelong habit, I'm afraid. To most people breakfast consists of coffee and cornflakes. To me it's coffee and the stock-market column.

'Still, in the interests of good manners, I'll make an exception just this once...' Holding her gaze, his blue eyes twinkling, he proceeded to fold up the newspapers and toss them one by one on the floor.

Then he nodded towards the now-revealed packet of cornflakes. 'That's in your honour. See what an effort I made?'

There was even a carton of milk and a cereal bowl and spoon. Charlotte pulled a face. 'My,' she observed, 'you must really be trying to impress me.'

'Indeed I am.' Jett sat back in his chair and eyed her across the table for a moment, admiring her neat slim figure dressed in a simple blue cotton dress. 'But then impressing young ladies is something I always enjoy.'

Yes, that was what she'd heard. Jett Ashton, the great seducer!

Charlotte narrowed her eyes as she poured herself some coffee. 'Well, I can't think why you'd want to impress me,' she observed coolly.

'Perhaps I'm trying to win you round, so you'll do as I wish.' He pushed the packet of cornflakes and the milk towards her. 'Don't be shy,' he invited. 'Help yourself.'

Charlotte did so, making a point of detaching her gaze from his. Had she imagined it or had there been a hint of sexual challenge in his tone as he'd made that remark about her doing as he wished? An unexpected twinge of awareness had gone

through her and she felt irked at herself as much
as at him. She had no business responding to him
in such a manner. On every level, including the
sexual one, she found him abominable.

Pouring cornflakes into her bowl, she glanced up
at him again. 'As I warned you last night, I may
not do as you wish, so this little get-together may
prove to be a waste of time.'

'Let's hope not.' Lifting his mug, Jett took a
mouthful of coffee. 'One thing I can't stand is
wasting time.'

Charlotte didn't doubt it. Time, after all, was
money. A man like him would keep a very strict
eye on the clock. As he'd admitted, he didn't even
take time off to have a proper breakfast!

Yet all the same, as she watched him across the
table, it struck Charlotte that he looked a little different today. More relaxed, less severe, though it
was probably just the casual clothes. Previously,
she had only ever seen him in formal business suits.

'So, how's your charge? Did he get off to nursery
school OK?' Jett laid down his coffee-mug and
glanced across at her. 'From what I've seen of him
he seems like a bright little chap.'

Charlotte smiled sceptically to herself. He really
was trying to win her round. For Ellen had told her
he took no interest in the child. In fact, he had only
ever met Lucas a couple of times.

But she said nothing. None of that was any of
her business. Instead, she nodded, smiling warmly
as she thought of little Lucas, the affection she felt
for him shining from her eyes. 'Yes, he is a bright
child. And he just adores nursery school. I think
he'd happily spend all day there.'

'Bring him round some time.' Jett continued to watch her. 'I'm sure he'd enjoy himself here at the manor.'

The invitation surprised Charlotte—he really was out to lure her! She answered with a smile, 'That's very kind of you. He hasn't been round since your uncle Oscar died. And he does love it here, particularly the conservatory.' She laughed as she told him, 'He calls it the jungle.'

'Then bring him tomorrow and let him spend some time here. Any time that suits you. I leave it up to you.'

Such magnanimity! Though Charlotte wasn't taken in. He'd probably contrive to be out if she did bring Lucas round! Ellen had told her he had no time for children.

But again she simply nodded and took a mouthful of her cornflakes. 'We'll see,' she told him. Then she caught his eye and added meaningfully, 'After all, we don't even know yet if I'll be staying on at the manor myself.'

'Oh, I think you will.' He regarded her for a moment, his expression irritatingly reflecting the absolute certainty in his voice. Then he asked her, 'So, how long are you staying on to look after Lucas? You said it was only a temporary arrangement.'

'It is. I'll probably only be needed for a couple of weeks more. Ellen's come to an arrangement with some girl from the village. All they have to do is fix a definite date when she can start.'

'And then what happens to you?'

'I have a job waiting for me in London. I'm due to start in three weeks' time.'

'So, you'll be leaving the area.'

'Yes, I'm afraid so. But London's where I'm normally based. I have a small flat in Finsbury Park,' she told him. 'A friend's been looking after it,' she added unnecessarily.

'I see. No doubt you'll be glad to get back to the big city?'

'In a way. I like London. But I'll miss Ted and Ellen. We've grown quite close,' she enlarged, just to annoy him. 'After all, I've seen them every day of the year I've been here.'

'Some might say that was good cause to be glad to see the back of them.' Jett smiled a slow, sarcastic smile. 'Personally, I admire your staying power.'

Charlotte had expected that response, but still it irked her. Ellen and Ted had been kind to her, especially Ellen, and they just didn't deserve Jett's constant hostility and criticism.

She straightened in her chair. 'By the way, I told Ellen that you claimed to have no knowledge of the fact that I was staying here.' She tilted her chin at Jett defiantly. 'She said Ted definitely telexed your New York office to ask for your OK on the arrangement. When he heard nothing back, they just assumed you had no objections.'

'Then that must be what happened. The fault is mine.' Again the sarcasm was heavy in his voice. 'Who am I to doubt the word of Ted?'

Charlotte pursed her lips, biting back her irritation. They hadn't even started discussing what they were here for, namely the terms under which she might agree to stay on, but already she felt certain it was going to be a waste of time. She didn't want to stay on. Not on any terms. Life under the same roof as Jett Ashton would be much too unpleasant.

But at least she might as well finish her cornflakes! She took another mouthful and chewed for a moment before telling him,

'By the way, Ellen and Ted have offered me the sofa bed in the sitting room if you and I should fail to reach an agreement.'

'Then let's hope we don't.' Jett smiled unexpectedly. 'Sofa beds in my experience are invariably devilishly uncomfortable.'

As he met her eyes, Charlotte was about to smile back at him. To be truthful, that small detail had occurred to her, too! But then he continued, still in that deceptively light tone,

'What a pity they don't have a house with a spare room. Ah, well, perhaps that's something they'll be able to rectify soon.'

Charlotte felt a jarring sense of understanding as a picture sprang to mind of Ellen's face that morning when Charlotte had told her that Jett was back at the manor.

'Oh, lord,' Ellen had moaned. 'I'll bet he's come to evict us.' Tears had sprung to her eyes. 'What on earth will we do?'

'Don't be silly,' Charlotte had soothed her. 'Why on earth would he evict you? He doesn't need the Coach House. And surely not even Jett would do anything so spiteful!'

But now, as she looked into his harsh, uncaring face, she wasn't so sure of that earlier assessment. She felt a flicker of concern as she met his gaze across the table. She'd always felt the family feud was none of her business, but she couldn't allow that last remark of his to pass without comment.

Charlotte straightened in her seat. 'Is it your intention,' she put to him, 'to throw your cousin and his family out of their house?'

Jett looked back at her without a flicker. 'The house you refer to as theirs happens to belong to me.'

'But they live in it and it's the only house they've got.' She repeated her demand. 'Would you really throw them out?'

Jett raised dark eyebrows, a harsh look in his eyes. 'I really don't think that my plans for the Coach House are what you and I are here to discuss.'

'I see. So you have plans?' That did sound ominous. 'And do those plans,' Charlotte insisted, 'involve evicting Ellen and Ted?'

'What we're here to discuss...' It was as though she had not spoken. He cut right through her like secateurs through thin wire. 'What we're here to discuss is your staying on at the manor—and what arrangement we can come to that would be acceptable to us both.'

As he paused and fixed her with eyes of blue ice, Charlotte simply felt her anger grow more intense. I shall never come to an arrangement with this man, she thought grimly. I simply couldn't bear to be anywhere near him!

She sat very still and said in a low voice, 'Would you really throw them out on the street? Your own cousin and his wife and their three-year-old child?' At the thought of little Lucas, her anger grew tenfold. 'How could you do that?' she demanded. 'How could you deprive that little boy of his home?'

Jett continued to ignore her as though she hadn't spoken. He sat back in his seat. 'What I would suggest is this. In return for free bed and board here at the manor, I simply want you to see to it that the house is properly run . . .'

As he paused, Charlotte was on the point of rising to her feet and telling him straight that she wasn't interested in hearing the rest. She felt so angry she just wanted to get up and walk out.

But something made her stay—the beginnings of an idea that was starting to take shape in her head. Brain buzzing, she sat back and listened as he continued,

'As you know, now that Mrs Kibble, my uncle's old housekeeper, has retired, the only domestic help we have is the gardener, old Bill Willis, and a part-time girl who comes in every morning to do some cleaning. So that leaves us with a couple of gaps to be filled.'

He leaned forward suddenly. 'And I would like you to do the filling.'

'Personally, do you mean?'

Did he want her to be his skivvy?

Jett caught her eye and held it. 'Not, personally, no. I think that would be rather a waste of your talents.'

He continued to hold her gaze, smiling with amusement, and to Charlotte's dismay she felt again the tingle of awareness. It's those eyes of his and the way he looks at me, she thought crossly.

He was continuing, 'All I want you to do is just oversee things until the new housekeeper is installed. Perhaps you could arrange for the part-time girl to come full-time for a while—and you'll need to hire another, permanent full-time girl, someone who can do the cooking in the meantime.

'Normally, the new housekeeper will do all the cooking. I've already hired a new housekeeper— Bill Willis's sister. But she's currently employed at some castle up in Scotland and won't be free for a couple of weeks.'

'You've found a new housekeeper already?' Charlotte was impressed by his efficiency. Mrs Kibble had only retired a couple of weeks ago. 'My,' she observed archly, 'you're well organised.'

'I'm *extremely* well organised—as I shall expect you to be, also.' He said it with a smile, but the remark had an edge like a razor.

Then he added on a softer note, 'Not that you'll have much to do. All I ask is that you organise things so that over the next couple of weeks I'm provided with three edible meals a day and the house is kept reasonably clean and tidy.'

He smiled. 'I don't think that ought to over-stretch you.'

Charlotte was thinking the same. In fact, it ought to be a doddle. It sounded as though she'd have plenty of time left for painting.

But the urge was still strong to turn him down flat. It might *sound* easy enough, but working for Jett Ashton, when it actually came down to it, would never be easy. That was something she knew as instinctively as breathing. But what stopped her saying no was that niggling idea that with every minute was unfolding with more certainty in her head.

He was watching her, waiting. 'So, what do you say?'

Charlotte took a deep breath. Quite frankly, she longed to tell him, 'I'd rather opt for Ellen's sofa bed and some decent company.' But she hesitated. 'I'll have to think about it,' she told him, playing for time.

'Then go ahead and think about it.' In one mouthful, he drained his coffee cup. 'But I'll need your answer by the time you've finished those cornflakes. You see, if you turn me down, I'll have to make other arrangements.'

Charlotte laid down her spoon and stared into her plate. Her brain was going round in circles. Then she glanced up with narrowed eyes. 'You never answered me, you know. Would you really throw Ellen and Ted out of their house? Would you really put that little boy of theirs out on the street?'

The blue eyes looked right through her as though she hadn't spoken. 'What's the matter? You're not eating. Have you lost your appetite?'

Again Charlotte felt the surge of anger whip through her and the accompanying desire to turn him down flat. But she stopped herself. First, she had to know the answer to her question. She glared at Jett. 'You still haven't answered me,' she said.

'Haven't I?'

He was infuriating. Charlotte gritted her teeth. 'Would you really throw Ellen and Ted out of the Coach House? It's a simple question. Yes or no?'

Jett had leaned back in his chair, the blue eyes suddenly shadowed. He seemed to be considering how to answer her question.

Then in a calm voice, he told her, 'You want a categorical yes or no? Well, since there's no way I could possibly give you a categorical no, I suggest you draw your own conclusions.'

So, now she had her answer. If it wasn't no, it must be yes. And, now that she had her answer, Charlotte knew what she must do.

She looked into his face, feeling a twist of uneasiness. She knew what she must do, but she did not relish it in the slightest.

Glancing away, avoiding his eyes, she took a deep breath. The plain fact was that she couldn't just walk away. For she wouldn't just be walking away from Jett. She'd also be walking away from the opportunity to try and change his mind about evicting Ted and Ellen. She might very well fail anyway, but she knew she had to try.

Steeling herself, she looked up at him. 'OK,' she agreed. 'I'll stay.'

Jett met her eyes and held them in silence for a moment. Then a slow wicked smile began to curl round his lips.

'I thought so,' he observed, his smile growing broader. 'You fancy yourself as a go-between between me and Ted and Ellen. Brave girl,' he added with an amused lift of his eyebrows.

Then, as she stared back at him in silence, a little annoyed that he'd read her so easily, he let his eyes glance over her like caressing fingers, making her wonder with a flutter of panic if she ought to withdraw her agreement.

And she had a very strong feeling that he was spot-on as he added, 'I think we're going to have an extremely interesting couple of weeks.'

CHAPTER THREE

'TELL me a story about Bertie Rabbit going to the jungle. About lions and tigers and snakes and crocodiles.' Lucas's bright brown eyes sparkled. 'Can you, Charlotte?'

Charlotte smiled down at the child. 'If you want me to,' she told him. Then she nodded and took his hand. 'Let's find a quiet corner and I'll tell you a story about Bertie Rabbit in the jungle.'

The two of them were in the conservatory at Penforth Manor. Charlotte had decided to take Jett at his word and that morning when she'd gone to the Coach House to pick up Lucas and take him off to his nursery group she'd mentioned to Ellen what Jett had told her.

'He says Lucas is welcome to visit any time, and since it looks as though it's going to rain this afternoon and we won't be able to play out in the garden, I thought I might take him up to the manor this afternoon. That is,' she'd added quickly, 'if it's all right with you.'

Ellen had hesitated for just a moment. 'I don't know if Ted will approve,' she'd said, wrinkling her brow and frowning a little. Then she'd sighed. 'But I'm sure it can't do any harm and Lucas does love it so up at the manor.'

'I'm sure it won't do any harm,' Charlotte had assured her. 'After all, it's such a big house he and Jett probably won't even meet!'

Besides, Jett will probably keep out of the way, she'd thought privately. For she suspected that what Ellen had told her was right and Jett Ashton had precious little time for children!

'OK.' With a smile, Ellen had agreed. Then she'd called to Lucas, who was finishing his breakfast in the kitchen. 'Guess what? Charlotte's going to take you up to the manor this afternoon. What do you think about that? Do you think it's a good idea?'

Lucas had been in no doubt that it was an excellent idea. He'd leapt from his stool, his little face beaming. 'Can we visit the jungle, Charlotte? Please!'

And, of course, that was where they were now, in the huge conservatory that Lucas always called 'the jungle'. Which was a pretty good name for it, Charlotte had always reckoned. With its tall, exotic palm trees and banks of trailing ferns, it was a magical place, full of mystery and wonder.

'Come up here beside me.' She had seated herself against the cushions of the comfy cane sofa that stood in one corner. Then as the little boy clambered up beside her, she tousled his hair and slipped an arm around him. 'Now, let's see,' she said smiling. 'Where shall we begin . . . ?'

Half an hour later, to the friendly accompaniment of raindrops pattering on the glass all around them, Charlotte was coming to the end of her story.

'And so,' she concluded, 'Bertie Rabbit and the tiger remained firm friends ever after.'

'Did Bertie Rabbit go back to the jungle to visit him?' With shining brown eyes the child looked up at her.

Charlotte gave him a squeeze and kissed the top of his head. 'Oh, I think so,' she said. 'In fact, I'm sure of it.' Then she winked at him. 'But we'll keep that story for another day.'

'I can't wait to hear it.' Suddenly, a deep voice had spoken. Charlotte whirled round with a start to see Jett standing in the doorway.

She felt herself flush. How long had he been standing there?

But before she could say a word, he'd stepped into the conservatory, his hands in the pockets of his blue suit trousers. 'Hi, Lucas,' he said. 'Do you remember me? I'm your uncle Jett. How are you doing?'

Lucas nodded a little uncertainly. 'Hello,' he answered. Then he glanced up at Charlotte, unsure of what to do next.

Charlotte gave him a quick, reassuring little hug. 'Why don't you go and play with your train?' she suggested, nodding towards the train set he'd been playing with earlier. 'You can pretend it's taking Bertie Rabbit to visit Tiger in the jungle.'

Lucas nodded enthusiastically at that suggestion. He slipped down from the cane sofa. 'OK,' he beamed.

And now it was Charlotte who was wondering what to do next. As Jett continued to stand there, hands in pockets, she shifted uncomfortably in her seat.

His sudden appearance had thrown her a little. It annoyed her to think he'd been spying on her and Lucas. But through her annoyance she was also uncomfortably aware of that increasingly familiar and rather pleasurable tingle as she looked up into the smiling sapphire-blue eyes.

She found herself saying a little breathlessly, 'I hope you don't mind me bringing Lucas here? After all, you did say I could.'

'Then how could I possibly mind?'

'You might have forgotten.'

'Like I supposedly forgot that you were staying here?' Jett smiled as he said it. 'I can assure you,' he told her, 'I really don't suffer from a defective memory.'

There was a hint of teasing in his eyes as he looked at her and not an ounce of hostility in his tone of voice for once.

'In fact,' he added, 'I'm glad you took me up on my offer.'

It's for Lucas's sake, Charlotte found herself thinking, surprised and pleased that he should show such sensitivity in the child's presence. But, foolishly, she also felt a twinge of disappointment that this display of charm was not exclusively for her.

She pushed the feeling from her, a little alarmed that she'd even felt it. Surely the last thing she wanted was Jett Ashton trying to charm her?

She glanced airily around her. 'We've had a lovely afternoon. Lucas really likes it here.'

'I'm glad.'

As he spoke, Jett was stepping through the doorway and coming towards her across the tiled floor. And Charlotte felt her heart stutter as he came to a halt just inches from the edge of the cane sofa where she was sitting.

'Do you mind if I join you for a few minutes?' he asked.

'Of course not.'

She shook her head, but her stomach had tightened nervously. Was he planning to sit beside her on the sofa? At the thought she felt her body burn. It was a very small sofa.

But even as Charlotte contemplated what she would do if he did, he was reaching for one of the nearby cane armchairs, swivelling it round to face her and seating himself on it.

He leaned back and regarded her. 'So, tell me,' he asked her, 'where did you learn to tell such good stories?'

'What stories?'

All at once her mind had gone blank and her heart was beating very strangely. She had never known her heart to beat this way before.

It was because he was so close and facing her so squarely. She felt peculiarly overwhelmed by him. As though he might swallow her.

Doing her best to fight the feeling, she asked again, 'What stories?'

'Stories like the one you were telling Lucas.' Jett tossed her a wink. 'I'm afraid I'm guilty of eavesdropping. I arrived quite a little while ago. I heard most of your story.'

'It was meant for Lucas.' Charlotte felt foolishly defensive. 'It wasn't meant for adult ears.'

'Nevertheless, these adult ears rather enjoyed it.' He tilted his head to one side and looked at her, making something inside her melt like jelly. 'You're a many talented girl, it would seem. Not only can you draw, you can also tell stories.'

'It's nothing.'

Charlotte was starting to get her heartbeat back under control again. She was doing this by sitting well back in her chair, breathing slowly and avoiding looking at his eyes. It was the power of those blue eyes, she'd decided, that threw her.

She continued, focusing carefully on the bridge of his nose, 'When I was a hospital nurse and working on the children's ward, and when I had time, which wasn't often, I used to tell the children stories.'

That was when it had all started, she might have added. That had been the beginning of her ambition to write story-books for children.

'You do it well. I'd say you're a natural story-teller.' Jett smiled as he added, 'I certainly enjoyed the one I heard.'

'Really?'

She shrugged as though the compliment meant nothing, but in spite of herself she'd felt a small flicker of pleasure. It was probably not so, but he'd said it as though he'd meant it. In her confusion she forgot to keep her eyes on his nose.

And it was definitely a mistake. As her gaze strayed to his eyes again, she heard him say, 'So, what other talents do you have?' But she was lost in those blue eyes again, her heart beating like a drum.

Then to make matters worse he suddenly leaned towards her. 'One day we must have a proper chat, you and I. I suspect you're a very interesting girl.'

It was just another line. Charlotte knew that. But that look in his eyes was making her quite dizzy. She struggled to think of something that would fend him off—and that was when, in a sudden flash, she remembered.

She sat up straight. 'Oh, I forgot to tell you . . . Some girl rang—twice—while you were out. I'm afraid she didn't leave any message.'

'Some girl?'

Jett appeared only mildly interested—a fact which, to Charlotte's dismay, did not displease her. Not that it meant anything, she told herself swiftly. It simply confirmed that what she'd suspected was true—that he had a string of girlfriends who called him up all the time. Girls whom he seduced with those blue bedroom eyes of his and lines about how interesting he suspected they were.

Charlotte watched him with a welcome twinge of disapproval as he asked her, 'Didn't she even leave a name?'

'She declined.' Charlotte couldn't resist a slightly knowing smile. 'But she seemed very anxious to know who I was. I simply told her I was the hired help.'

'How very modest of you.'

'Not modest. Just accurate. Anyway, she said she'd ring back later.'

'In that case, I shall wait for her call with bated breath.'

As he smiled an amused smile, Charlotte looked into his face, suddenly irked by this display of careless indifference. All at once, she felt sympathy for his poor girlfriend, who would probably be rather hurt if she knew how little he cared.

Just to annoy him, she added, 'She sounded extremely keen to reach you, so I suspect you won't have very long to wait.'

'That's a relief.' He smiled cynically. 'As you already know, I don't have much of a taste for waiting.'

And then he proceeded to change the subject.

'But let's talk about something far more pressing . . .' He leaned back in his seat. 'What progress have you made with sorting out the domestic arrangements?'

'I've made very good progress, as a matter of fact.'

Charlotte met his gaze with a confident smile and felt herself relax inside. She liked it better now that he had sat back in his seat, and that the conversation had taken a more businesslike turn.

'Annie,' she continued, 'the girl who comes part-time at the moment, is more than happy to work full-time for as long as she's needed. And I've found another full-time girl who can cook as well as clean. Mrs Kibble recommended her. She's starting tomorrow.'

'So, you spoke to Mrs Kibble? That was a smart move.'

'I thought if anyone knew the right person, she probably would.'

She ignored the compliment, though, annoyingly, it had pleased her. It was just another of those lines he enjoyed handing out, like the one about her being an interesting person.

Studiedly immune to him, she continued, 'The new girl's worked here before. She did a couple of weeks once to help Mrs Kibble out when Annie was off ill with flu. So, she knows the house. That's always a help.'

Jett nodded. 'It sounds as though you've done a good job.' His eyes drifted over her. 'Congratulations,' he said.

Charlotte nodded in acknowledgement, holding on tight to her immunity as those drifting blue eyes sent a shiver of pleasure through her.

Matter-of-factly, she agreed, 'Yes, I feel quite pleased.'

And she did. She had spent all morning on the phone, but it had turned out to be a highly fruitful morning's work.

But then Jett smiled a warning smile. 'Now all you have to do is ensure that Annie and the new girl do a good job, too.'

'I have no doubt that they will. Both of them are good girls. I'm sure they'll do an excellent job.'

'That's fine, then. In that case, you have nothing to worry about.'

'Worry about. What do you mean worry about?' That warning look in his eyes was suddenly making her feel a little uneasy. 'What are you trying to say?' she wanted to know.

'I'm not trying to say anything. I'm just reminding you that you're responsible for the girls' performance. If they don't perform well, I'll expect you to deal with it.'

'Deal with it how?'

'That's really up to you.' He held her eyes a moment. Then he shrugged as he added, 'The simplest way would be to fire them and hire someone else.'

'Fire them? Just like that?' What a ruthless suggestion! Charlotte made no effort to disguise her disapproval. 'Is that what you do—fire people just like that?'

'If they don't do their jobs. Why, what would you suggest?'

'I would suggest giving them a second chance.' Her grey eyes sparked at him. 'Surely, everyone's entitled to a second chance? After all, we all make mistakes.'

'That may be your philosophy, but I'm afraid it's not mine. Giving people second chances can be a costly business.' He smiled a smile so callous that Charlotte wondered if it was real. Did he mean what he was saying or was he just enjoying shocking her? She still hadn't decided as he went on to elaborate, 'It's better to weed out the failures before they do too much damage.'

Charlotte very nearly said, 'I'm glad I don't work for you!' That was at least one thing she *was* sure about! But then she suddenly remembered that she did work for him—even if only in a temporary capacity! Though there was one thing to be thankful for. She wouldn't be losing any sleep over the possibility of being weeded out. Quite frankly, he could weed her out any time he liked!

She regarded him flintily, just in case he was serious. 'We're talking about people's livelihoods, about depriving them of their income. They're not just a bunch of weeds to be tossed on the scrap heap.'

Not that he would understand about that, she reminded herself silently. The fear of losing his job, of ending up on the scrap heap, was not one that Jett Ashton had never had to contemplate. All his life, he'd had everything handed to him on a plate. Ellen had told her. Jett had been born lucky.

'So, if it's all the same to you,' she added, narrowing her eyes at him, 'I won't be adopting your rather callous philosophy. If either of the girls I've hired falls down on the job, I'll do things my way and give them a second chance.'

Jett shrugged again uncaringly. 'That's entirely up to you. All I demand is that you make sure the jobs get done—that the house is kept clean and the meals get cooked on time. How you do it is your own affair.'

'Good. You can rest assured everything will be done.' Even if I have to do it myself, she was about to add. But she stopped herself in time. That would be a bit rash.

And suddenly, though she was continuing to smile at him confidently, Charlotte was aware of a small twinge of foreboding. Had she perhaps let herself in for a little more than she'd originally bargained for?

But that was just silly, she assured herself hurriedly. Annie and the new girl weren't about to let her down.

It was at that very moment that the telephone rang.

Jett rose from the chair. 'I'll get that,' he told her. His eyes held a look of teasing amusement as he added, 'Naturally, from tomorrow, there'll be someone else to answer it for me.'

It was probably his girlfriend, anyway, the one who'd phoned him twice already, Charlotte thought as she watched him head back into the drawing-room with that easy arrogant gait he had. He expects to be waited on hand and foot, she thought, and silently put up a heartfelt prayer that Annie and the new girl would live up to the faith she'd put in them.

Then she rose to her feet and crossed the tiled conservatory to where Lucas was playing in total absorption with his train set.

She knelt down beside him. 'How's it going?' she asked him. 'Are you managing to find your way through the jungle?'

Lucas nodded. 'We nearly got eaten by some crocodiles. But Tiger came along just in time and saved us.'

Charlotte laughed and tousled his hair affectionately. 'Good for Tiger. I hope you remembered to say thank-you.'

'It's for you.' Jett had reappeared in the doorway. 'It's Annie. She says she wants to talk to you.'

'For me? What does she want?'

Charlotte had spun round to look at him. Good grief, she was thinking. Don't say I spoke too soon!

Jett simply shrugged. 'She didn't say what she wanted, just that she wanted to speak to you.' Then he added, clearly enjoying the sudden alarm in her face, 'I'd hurry if I were you. It sounded urgent.'

Sadist! He was enjoying this! Charlotte headed for the door. Then she paused and caught Jett's eye, casting a quick glance at the child. 'Will you keep an eye on Lucas, please, while I'm out of the room?'

'Yes, I think I can manage that.' He stood aside to let her past. 'Now run along,' he urged her. 'I told you it sounded urgent.'

Cursing him silently, Charlotte hurried into the drawing-room, crossed to the phone and snatched up the receiver. 'Hello? Annie?' she said a little nervously, wondering what on earth was coming next.

But she needn't have worried. A little breathlessly, Annie answered. 'Miss Channing, I'm just calling to check that you want me to start at the same time as usual tomorrow morning. Usually, I start just at the back of eight.'

'That's fine. Just as long as you're in time to prepare Mr Ashton's breakfast as we agreed.' Charlotte smiled with relief. 'I look forward to seeing you then.'

She laid the phone down again, feeling her heart rate return to normal. Just for a moment back then she'd almost had kittens. The most horrible scenario had flashed before her eyes. There she'd been, down on her knees, scrubbing floors like some latter-day Cinderella, with Jett standing over like a male ugly sister! Wouldn't he just have loved that! she thought to herself as she headed back to the conservatory.

But these thoughts fled the moment she reached the open doorway.

While she'd been gone, Jett had re-seated himself in his armchair. And now, to Charlotte's surprise, standing at his knee, proudly showing him his train engine, stood a chattering, bright-eyed little Lucas.

The scene caused her to pause for a moment in the doorway. Funny, she thought, I'd expected him to ignore the child. But he was far from ignoring him. He was smiling down at him, apparently enjoying the exchange every bit as much as Lucas.

That's nice, she thought with unexpected pleasure. It looked as though Lucas had made a new friend.

Then as the child went off to play with his train again, Jett demanded over his shoulder, 'Everything OK? No unexpected problems with Annie, I hope?'

'Everything's perfect.' Charlotte stepped into the room, her eyes shooting daggers into the back of his head. She knew perfectly well he would have enjoyed a rather less positive answer!

'Good,' he responded. 'I'll bet that's a relief.'

Charlotte ignored that remark and glanced at her watch. Then she addressed herself to Lucas. 'I think we ought to be going. Your mummy will be home soon and she'll be wanting to hear what you've been up to. Come on. I'll help you gather up that train set.'

'He can leave it here if he likes, and come and play with it whenever he wants to.' Jett paused and turned to ask Lucas, 'Would you like that?'

'Oh, yes, please.' Lucas nodded enthusiastically. 'I'd like to come back.'

'That's settled, then.' Unhurriedly, Jett rose to his feet. Then, with one of his amused smiles, he turned to face Charlotte. 'About dinner this evening ... I've arranged to eat out. So you won't have to put yourself to the trouble of cooking dinner for me.'

I wasn't planning to, anyway. Charlotte resisted the urge to say it. Yes, she was thinking, I really have let myself in for something. If these girls let me down, I really have had it. The Cinderella scenario would all too quickly come true!

But she revealed none of these dark thoughts. Instead, she faked a warm smile. 'I can assure you,' she told him, 'it would have been no trouble.'

'Good. I'm glad to hear that.' He smiled back at her with an amused smile. Then he glanced down at Lucas. 'I hope to see you again soon.'

Charlotte held out her hand for the child. 'Come on, Lucas. Let's go.' Then she hesitated. 'Thanks for your hospitality,' she told Jett. At least, she couldn't fault his generosity as far as Lucas was concerned.

'My pleasure.' Jett simply nodded and paused to watch them go. But then as Lucas stepped in front of her into the drawing-room, he added, causing Charlotte to turn and face him once more, 'He's a nice kid. This evening I shall make a point of congratulating his father on having such a lovely young son.'

Charlotte felt her eyes widen. 'You're seeing Ted this evening?' Somehow she didn't like the sound of that at all.

'We're having dinner together at a restaurant in the village. Somewhere discreet where we can talk together in private.' He smiled the smile of a crocodile contemplating its next victim. 'It ought to be an interesting evening.'

I'll bet! Charlotte turned away with a sick feeling in her stomach. Were Ellen's fears about to come true? she was wondering. Was the purpose of this discreet dinner to serve an eviction notice on Ted and throw the whole family out of the Coach House?

As she headed down the long, curving driveway with Lucas, her heart was suddenly filled with a fierce sense of outrage. What a two-faced snake Jett was! Just a matter of a few minutes ago he'd been chatting to Lucas with every pretence of affection—and all the while he'd been planning to make the poor child homeless.

Well, it wasn't going to happen! She clenched her fists determinedly. Before he could speak to Ted, she was going to confront him and demand that he abandon this evil plan of his.

Jett Ashton thought he could get away with anything. But this time he hadn't reckoned on her!

CHAPTER FOUR

CHARLOTTE had stormed back to the manor house, hyped-up and ready to confront him, only to discover that Jett had disappeared.

She cursed to herself. Where the devil had he gone? It was nearly six o'clock and, according to Ellen, his dinner with Ted was arranged for eight. Would he be coming back to Penforth Manor first or going straight to the restaurant?

The little chat she'd had with Ellen when she'd dropped Lucas off at the Coach House had simply doubled her conviction that she had to confront him. For Ellen's fears were the same as her own.

'I'm sure this is it. He's going to throw us out of the Coach House.' Ellen had been so upset she could barely speak.

Charlotte had tried to comfort her. 'Maybe not,' she'd told her, laying a hand on Ellen's arm. 'Maybe he wants to talk to Ted about something else.'

She didn't believe it, but it wasn't impossible, after all. And she had to say something to stop Ellen's tears.

Then, frowning, she'd added, 'I'm going to speak to him. I don't know if it'll help, but I'm going to have a shot.' She'd squeezed Ellen's arm. 'So, keep your fingers crossed.'

Her own fingers were crossed now as she paced the floor in her room, ears pricked impatiently for the sound of Jett's car. It was getting close to seven o'clock and there was still no sign of him.

She kept glancing at her watch, the tension in her growing. She knew Jett would be furious at her for daring to confront him, but, though she was nervous, she had no intention of letting that stop her. She couldn't just stand by and watch Jett make Lucas and his parents homeless.

It was precisely seven o'clock when she heard a car draw up outside. Charlotte darted to the window that overlooked the driveway. And it was Jett, all right. She watched from behind the curtains as the door of the sleek white Jaguar swung open and his tall dark figure slid arrogantly out. Then he was striding on long, muscular legs to the front door.

Charlotte stood back from the window and took a deep breath. He looked as though he'd already changed for the evening—he was wearing a dark semi-formal suit—so what he'd probably do now was go through to the drawing-room and pour himself an aperitif. A single malt whisky to sharpen his appetite for his evil work.

She squared her shoulders and touched the neck of her turquoise blouse, fighting back a sudden surge of nerves. Then she smoothed her white skirt, tossed back her blonde hair and headed resolutely for the door.

Charlotte had been right about one thing. Jett was in the drawing-room. As she made her way downstairs she could hear the sound of music wafting through the half-open doorway. She nodded to herself. Beethoven, of course. That strong, forceful music suited him to a Te!

And she'd been right about another thing. As she stepped through the drawing-room door, he was just replacing the stopper on a crystal whisky decanter.

He glanced up without surprise, almost as though he'd been expecting her. 'Would you care for a drink?' he asked.

He'd discarded his jacket—it lay over a nearby armchair—to reveal a fine white shirt and burgundy silk tie. And he looked quite stunning, dressed in these strong contrasting colours. They enhanced his own dramatic dark looks.

Charlotte felt a surge of illogical pleasure go through her. He might be a snake, but he was a feast for the eyes!

Jett straightened and turned to her with a look of amusement. 'Was that a yes or a no?' he enquired.

Charlotte pulled herself together. 'I suppose it was a yes.' What on earth was the matter with her? she asked herself sharply. Had she never seen a good-looking man before?

Jett reached for another whisky glass and poured a generous measure, then quickly splashed some soda into both of the glasses. 'Shall we sit?' he suggested, as Charlotte stepped forward to accept hers.

'OK.' As she looked into his face, she found herself answering her earlier question.

Of course, she'd seen plenty of good-looking men before. But none, she had to confess, half as good-looking as Jett Ashton. In the looks department he was definitely in a class of his own.

But then he was in a class of his own in every department, Charlotte reminded herself crisply as

she followed him across the room. In the ruth-
lessness department. In the heartlessness department. In the department of always putting
number one first. In all of these departments no
one could touch him.

He paused by a low coffee-table whose vast
square glass top was supported at each corner by
a crouching bronze lion and nodded at the group
of sofas and chairs that surrounded it.

'Make yourself comfortable,' he invited.

'Thank you.'

Charlotte seated herself on one of the two-seater
sofas, upholstered in heavy garnet-coloured
brocade, and watched as Jett seated himself in the
bigger sofa opposite. He thinks all we're going to
do is have a pleasant little chat, she thought, as she
leaned back against the cushions and took a sip of
her drink.

And for a moment it almost seemed a pity that
that wasn't so. It might be rather nice to spend a
civilised half-hour with him.

She rejected that thought instantly. It was quite
unworthy of her! But at least she could take the
time to pay him one small compliment.

'I don't usually care much for whisky,' she confessed, 'but I must say this is really excellent.'

'It's a twenty-year-old malt. I'm glad you like it.'
He smiled. 'I wouldn't dream of drinking anything
less to Beethoven.'

Charlotte smiled to herself. She'd even been right
about the whisky! All in all, she seemed to have
Jett Ashton pretty well summed up!

She cast him a polite smile. 'A grand drink for a grand composer.' Then her smile twisted slightly. 'Does all this grandness reflect your mood?'

'I'm in a pretty good mood.' He cast a superior smile back at her. 'And how about you? How's your mood?'

'Good enough.'

Charlotte fingered the clean-cut edges of her crystal whisky glass and was about to dive into what she'd come to say, when suddenly she paused, remembering something.

'Oh, by the way, that girl who phoned before . . .' She was aware of a strange clench inside her as she said it. 'Well, she phoned again. I'd just got back. It must have been about six o'clock.'

She found herself watching for his reaction.

There was no reaction. He simply said, 'How very tiresome. Did she leave her name this time?'

'She did, as a matter of fact. She said to tell you it was Imelda.'

This time, very definitely, there was a reaction. It was brief and fleeting, but Charlotte caught it. A shadow of dark displeasure touched his eyes and there was a sudden tightness round his jaw.

'I see,' he responded. 'I rather thought that's who it might be.'

That reaction had two simultaneous effects on Charlotte. She'd already been curious, and now she was doubly so. And, to her shame, she also felt peculiarly reassured.

'She said she'd call back,' she continued, trying to sound neutral. But all at once her curiosity was too strong to hold back. She cleared her throat. 'Who is Imelda?'

'No one.' Still with that dark look, Jett stared down into his whisky. 'Just a bit of the past that refuses to go away.'

Well, that was plain enough. Imelda was evidently an ex-girlfriend. And very much 'ex', judging by the expression on Jett's face. Charlotte was shocked by and rather ashamed of the sense of relief she felt.

He was looking up at her again, the dark look gone, the unedifying subject of Imelda dismissed.

'So what are your plans for the evening?' he wanted to know.

The question instantly jolted Charlotte back to the present and the reason why she was sitting here listening to Beethoven in his drawing-room. 'Nothing in particular,' she answered. 'Just dinner, then bed.' She paused. 'But actually I'm more interested in your evening.'

'My evening . . . ? Now I wonder what could possibly interest you about that?'

'Everything.' She leaned forward, ignoring his callous smile. He already knew precisely what she was getting at. Then she came straight to the point. 'Are you going to evict them?'

'Am I going to evict them?' Jett took a mouthful of his whisky and leaned back a little more comfortably against the cushions. Against the garnet brocade his jet-black hair was as sleek and glossy as a raven's wing.

Another smile touched his lips as he tilted his head at her in that gesture that, once before, Charlotte had found dangerously disarming. She had to fight rather hard not to find it so now.

Then he said, 'What makes you think that's any of your business?'

'I'm making it my business, whether you like it or not.' Charlotte spoke the words through impatiently clenched teeth. 'Well?' she demanded again. 'Are you planning to evict them?'

Jett's teeth weren't at all clenched. He smiled across at her quite calmly. 'If you mean do I plan to throw them all bodily out of the Coach House, you can relax for the moment. The answer is no.'

'But you intend to make them leave?'

'What I intend to do I shall do.' Just for a moment the callous humour left his eyes to be replaced by a flash of quick, cold warning. 'And I shall do it without any consultation with you.'

Charlotte said nothing for a moment. She had expected this reaction. She, too, leaned back against the cushions of her sofa, making an effort to appear as relaxed as he was.

She said, 'It would be a terrible thing, you know, if you were to put these poor people out of their home. How could you? They're your family. Think of little Lucas.'

There was a silence, the only sound one of the slower movements of the Beethoven rippling gently in the background. Jett took another mouthful of his whisky while Charlotte searched his expression desperately for even the tiniest hint of a reaction. But there was none. The blue eyes remained as hard as pick-axes. It would take more than she'd come up with so far to touch the heart of this man.

But as she racked her brains for some new strategy, he leaned forward, laid his glass down and totally surprised her with his next question.

'How are your rabbits? Have you been doing any more painting?'

'I did a bit this morning.'

She knew he was making fun of her. Hadn't he been highly amused by her 'rabbits with little hats on'?

She shrugged. 'I like to indulge myself when I have a bit of spare time.'

'I thought they were rather good, your rabbits,' he told her. 'Do you paint anything else, apart from rabbits?'

'Sometimes. Yes.'

She felt oddly tongue-tied. Normally, she loved nothing better than to talk about her painting when she found an interested listener. But that was the trouble. She suspected Jett wasn't really interested, that all he was doing was amusing himself at her expense.

She shrugged, trying to put him off. 'It's only a hobby.'

'Maybe so.' He tilted his head again. 'But you definitely have talent.'

Charlotte felt herself flush in a most ridiculous fashion. He had sounded totally sincere, not the faintest bit mocking, and her heart had glowed for a moment as though smiled upon by angels. Maybe she'd been wrong to believe he was trying to make fun of her.

'Perhaps you ought to think about trying to develop your talent, or maybe even making a bit of cash from it. I wouldn't be at all surprised if you were good enough, you know.'

'You think so? Really?'

Charlotte was perfectly sure that her cheeks were now the same shade of garnet as the sofa, and her heart was suddenly clattering inside her. She looked back at him and experienced an almost irresistible urge to confess that he'd hit the nail on the head. What he was suggesting was precisely what she hoped to do!

And she might very well have confided in him, but at that moment he dropped his gaze away. 'Funny,' he remarked, looking down at the carpet. 'Art seems to be a ubiquitous topic tonight. I'll be broaching the subject with Ted over dinner.'

'Oh?'

Charlotte's heart was still clattering inside her, but she was aware of the cool touch of disappointment. The subject had been changed. There were to be no confidences, after all.

Jett reached for his whisky glass that he'd placed earlier on the glass-topped table and took a long slow mouthful before replying.

'Yes,' he told her, and there was a sudden distance in his voice. 'Only the art under discussion over dinner will be of a rather more valuable variety.'

It was foolish, but that hurt. Charlotte felt the clattering stop. Just for a moment a chill wind blew through her heart.

Then she took a deep breath to chase away the feeling. 'I must say I'm surprised,' she observed in a calm tone. 'I hadn't expected that you and Ted would be talking about art.'

'Neither does Ted. He'll be as surprised as you are.' Jett smiled a mirthless smile and laid down his glass. 'Perhaps he underestimates my powers of observation. But though I may be an infrequent visitor to Penforth Manor, when a couple of valuable paintings disappear from the walls I'm afraid I do tend to notice.'

Charlotte had been watching him curiously, wondering what he was on about. But now she was beginning to think she understood. For she remembered well the paintings he was referring to, and she remembered also the reason why they'd disappeared.

'But there's no mystery,' she told him. 'Those paintings were sold in order to pay for repairs to the house. That's what your uncle Oscar told me. He was sad about it, but according to Ted there was no alternative.'

'Yes, that's the story.' There was a hard look on Jett's face. 'But, personally,' he added, 'I have a rather different theory.'

'What kind of theory?' The look on his face was chilling. Charlotte felt a shiver run the length of her spine. Then her grey eyes widened as a sudden thought struck her. 'Surely you're not suggesting that Ted stole those paintings?'

When he did not answer, but simply looked back at her unblinkingly, she exclaimed with a dismissive laugh, 'But that's ridiculous! Ted would never do such a thing! And, anyway,' she added, 'just look at the way he and Ellen live! Do they live as though they've got the proceeds of a couple of valuable paintings in their bank account?'

As she paused for breath, Jett smiled at her cynically. 'You're clearly not the world's best judge of character, but I must say you're commendably loyal to your friends.'

'Of course I am. What you're suggesting is ludicrous. They scarcely have two pennies to rub together between them! They scrimp and save constantly and they haven't had a holiday for years!'

'Poor things.'

'Yes, poor things.'

Particularly Ellen, Charlotte was thinking, as she glared into Jett's uncaring face. Ted—a little selfishly, it had often struck her—had the occasional fishing weekend at a friend's cabin in Cornwall, but poor Ellen hadn't had a day off for as long as she could remember. Did that sound like two people who were stealing paintings from Penforth Manor?

And Jett must be as aware as she was of their situation! She narrowed her eyes now as a new thought occurred to her and turned accusingly on Jett.

'I know what you're doing! You're inventing this whole thing in a cynical effort to blacken Ted's name. You're shameless! You're using this as an excuse to evict them!'

'I don't need an excuse. I can evict them any time I like.'

'But that's what you're doing, isn't it?' Suddenly, she was sure of it. 'Not only are you planning to evict them, you're going to ruin Ted's reputation in the process!'

The very idea was quite sickening. Charlotte sprang to her feet impatiently, suddenly unable to bear being in the same room as him.

And as she did so, she reached out to lay down her whisky glass—but in her state of shaking anger she misjudged the movement totally. The glass wobbled for a moment, then keeled over with a crash, spilling its contents over the glass-topped table.

Charlotte stopped in her tracks and glanced down in dismay at the pool of whisky spreading across the table top. 'What a mess. I'm sorry.' She looked round for some tissues. But there weren't any. She turned away. 'I'll get a cloth from the kitchen.'

'Don't worry about it.'

Suddenly, Jett was standing beside her, and out of nowhere a clean handkerchief had been dropped over the pool of whisky.

'Forget it,' he told her, bending down quickly to right the glass. 'It was just an accident. There's no harm done.'

It was true, no harm had been done to the table, but Charlotte was suddenly less certain about her own security. Jett's closeness was making her feel hopelessly vulnerable, and she didn't even have her anger any more to protect her. That had vanished as abruptly as a gambler's lucky streak the moment she had glanced round to find him standing at her side.

She averted her gaze. 'That was clumsy of me,' she mumbled. 'I really am most dreadfully sorry.'

There was no need to keep apologising. Charlotte was perfectly well aware of that. But she had to keep talking. She sensed a silence might be dangerous. And sorry was the only thing she could think of to say.

To her dismay, Jett did not answer, though she could feel his eyes on her and wished she could summon the strength to step away. But the more the silence stretched, the more immobile she became. She just stood there, listening to the slowly rising music, and waited for she knew not what, her poor heart frantic with anticipation.

Then, at last, Jett made a move. He reached out and took hold of her. And Charlotte found herself being swivelled round like a doll to face him, as the music all around them quickly gathered momentum.

Oh, dear, she thought helplessly, as her heart followed suit.

Then he spoke.

He said, 'I wish you'd stop worrying about Ted. What happens to Ted is in his own hands, not yours. And you can take my word for it, I have no intention whatsoever of inventing stories to blacken his name.'

At that moment Charlotte would have taken his word for anything. Her brain had gone blank. There were only two things she was aware of—the music that thundered and whirled in her head and the physical sensations that, in perfect time to the music, thundered and whirled around her nerve-ends.

For every inch of her, from the skin on her arm where he was touching her to the soles of her feet and the top of her head, was pulsing and burning as though she'd been plugged into an electric socket.

She shook her head and mumbled, 'That's OK, then.'

'You're not upset any more?'

'No, I'm not upset.'

If he didn't release her soon, she'd burn a hole in the carpet. She had a vision of herself, flames shooting from her hair, disappearing through the floorboards in a puff of smoke.

'I'm fine,' she assured him, quietly appalled at herself.

'Good. I promise you I didn't mean to upset you.' Jett smiled, and there was a cloudy look in his eyes. Suddenly, with his free hand, he reached up to touch her hair.

Charlotte felt herself stiffen and melt all at the same time. If she moved, she would fall down, she was absolutely certain. Her brain was suddenly a dazzle of flashing coloured lights.

Warning lights, one part of her brain was telling her. Star lights, the other, totally mesmerised, part answered. She felt rather more inclined to go along with the latter.

The hand in her hair had slipped round to the back of her neck, and it was unbearable the way his fingers were making her flesh tingle. It was becoming an effort just to carry on breathing.

The cloudy blue eyes were gazing down at her, pouring through her, filling her with temptation. And she could not resist them. As he drew her closer, Charlotte simply sighed and sank helplessly against him.

A moment later, just as the music reached its crashing climax, all the lights in Charlotte's head seemed to flash at once in a glorious kaleidoscope of brightness and colour. For that was the moment when he finally kissed her.

It was as though a hand had reached down and carried her up to heaven. Suddenly she was floating on a cloud of sheer bliss. And as he drew her even closer, she surrendered happily, thrilling at the fierce, gentle intimacy of his embrace.

And she burned all over in the most delicious fashion. Her lips, which clung to his, were crackling like a bushfire and her breasts, which were pressed hard and hot against his chest, had long ago succumbed to a helpless conflagration. And it was the most wonderful, most exciting sensation in the world.

With his hands Jett caressed her neck and her shoulders, the dip of her waist, the curve of her hips. And she shivered as his manhood thrust against her. The hard strength of him turned her muscles to water.

As his lips consumed her, her own lips responded with a hunger she'd never dreamed existed inside her. And as he kissed her lips, her cheeks, her neck, his tongue probing the warm soft recesses of her mouth, she shuddered and clung to him and kissed him back with all her strength.

Never before in her life had she known such yearning. She longed to sink to the floor with her arms around him and feel him strip the clothes from her flesh.

But that was to remain a fantasy, at least for the moment.

Suddenly, very gently, Jett was drawing away from her. 'I think we ought to call a halt,' he said gruffly. He smiled at her softly, raised her hand to his lips and kissed it. 'Or rather more than a shot of whisky's going to end up getting spilt.'

Charlotte felt herself flush, but not from shame or embarrassment. It was from sheer delight at the way he was looking down at her, and at the way he continued to hold her hand against his lips. His breath against her skin sent happy shivers through her. That look in his eyes was making her heart ache.

She smiled and nodded foolishly. 'You're right,' she said.

'But this is only a rain-check.' Softly, he kissed her hand again. 'I'd rather like to continue this some other time.'

Charlotte almost said, 'Me, too.' But she stopped herself in time. That might have been just a little too revealing, she decided. So, instead, she nodded mutely, glowed inside and said nothing.

'And now, I'd better go. As you know, I have an appointment.' He paused and kissed her lightly on the lips. 'And I don't want you to worry about that. Will you promise me you won't?'

A little dreamily, Charlotte nodded. 'OK. I promise.'

'And don't wait up for me. I'll probably be rather late. I've promised to drop in on an old friend after dinner.' He kissed her again. 'I'll see you in the morning.'

Then, with a final wink, he was disappearing out into the hallway, leaving Charlotte feeling as though she was floating on gossamer wings, so high that she was certain she would never come down again.

Feeling like a sleepwalker, the smile never leaving her face, Charlotte made herself some dinner, watched an hour of TV, then took herself off to bed for an early night. And she slept like a dream, though she had sobered just a little by the time the alarm went off just before eight next morning.

She lay for a moment against the warmth of the pillows and, focusing her thoughts, stared hard at the ceiling. Had yesterday evening really happened?

Oh, yes, it had definitely happened. The magical feeling still lingered. And though she suspected she was probably crazy, Charlotte didn't want to lose it. It was wonderful and she'd never felt anything like it in her life.

She showered quickly and pulled on some clothes—a pair of jeans and a navy blue turtle-neck sweater. She had to make herself presentable before Annie arrived. And she really must try to wipe the smirk off her face!

But the smirk remained. Never mind, she thought, laughing, maybe with an effort she might manage to dispose of it before the new girl, Sara, showed up. Sara, who would be working till later in the evenings, since she had the task of preparing Jett's dinners, wasn't due to start until eleven. Surely, she thought happily, she'd have stopped smirking by then!

It was as she was hurrying downstairs, full of nervous excitement at the thought of seeing Jett again, that the phone on the hall table began to ring. Charlotte halted in her tracks, a sudden sense of foreboding momentarily threatening to dent her good spirits.

At this hour, surely, the only person it could be was either Annie or Sara bringing her bad news. Her heart sank for an instant, then she shook the feeling from her as easily as a duck shook off water. Yesterday, such a prospect would have felt like a calamity, but today was different. Today she could cope with anything!

On unconcerned steps she headed for the phone, snatched up the receiver and held it to her ear.

'Hello?' she said. 'This is Penforth Manor.'

'Is Jett there? I have to speak to him.'

It was Imelda, Jett's girlfriend who'd rung so many times before. And this time she sounded quite hysterical.

'Just a minute. I'll get him.' Charlotte laid down the receiver. Suddenly there was a dull weight in the pit of her stomach.

She turned away to go and look for Jett—but suddenly there he was, coming down the staircase towards her.

Charlotte looked up into his smiling face, feeling her own face stiff and mask-like. 'It's for you,' she said. 'It's Imelda again.'

Jett took the receiver without a word of comment. But his smile had gone. Suddenly his face bore no expression.

On legs that had turned to straw, Charlotte hurried to the kitchen to fix herself some coffee and a bowl of cornflakes. But when she got there she just stood and stared at the wall.

She was still staring at it when Jett appeared in the open doorway behind her.

'It looks as though we're going to have a visitor,' he informed her. 'Imelda will be arriving this evening in time for dinner. I would be grateful if you'd make the necessary arrangements.'

Charlotte nodded without looking at him. Then she heard him walk away. And suddenly, as she stood there, still staring at the wall, her weight leaning heavily against the edge of the worktop, she felt totally immobilised by a sense of crushing disappointment.

In one bleak moment, all the magic had gone.

CHAPTER FIVE

AFTER picking half-heartedly at a bowl of corn-flakes, most of which she threw away, and forcing down a couple of mouthfuls of coffee, Charlotte climbed into her car to go and pick up Lucas. She was still in the process of trying to pull herself together.

She hadn't seen Jett again since his curt announcement that preparations should be made for Imelda's arrival. And she was glad. The thought of seeing him made her feel quite queasy. It didn't matter that she knew she was being absurdly silly.

For why should she care that his girlfriend was coming? The kisses they had exchanged last night meant nothing. On the contrary, as she kept reminding herself, she didn't even like him.

By the time she reached the Coach House she had managed to convince herself that she should actually be *glad* about this development. With Imelda around at least there'd be no danger of last night's folly ever recurring. She'd be safe, and surely that was what she wanted?

She was even more convinced after a few words with Ellen.

Ellen was looking drawn as she opened up the door to her. 'Come in,' she invited in her usual warm manner, though the smile that accompanied her words was a little shaky.

'Are you all right?' Charlotte was instantly filled with concern for her—and instantly guilty that since last night she'd barely given a thought to Ellen's problems.

'Don't worry', Jett had told her, implying there was nothing to worry about. And she'd been only too happy to believe him.

But she didn't feel happy now. 'What's happened?' she asked Ellen.

Ellen hesitated in the hallway, obviously very close to tears. She shook her head. 'I'm afraid Ted's dinner date with Jett turned out more or less as we'd feared . . .'

Charlotte's heart turned over sickly. 'Surely not!' she gasped. 'Surely he's not planning to evict you, after all?'

'I'm afraid he is. He hasn't set a date yet, but he told Ted to start looking around for a new place. I don't know what we're going to do. We're so short of money. We only just manage to make ends meet as it is.'

'But that's despicable! How can he do this?' Charlotte glanced through the kitchen doorway to where a happily oblivious Lucas was sitting at the kitchen table finishing his breakfast. And at the sight of the innocent child, so soon to be Jett's victim, she felt her sense of outrage double. 'The man is completely without morality!'

Ellen shook her head. 'It's terrible, Charlotte. He's been accusing poor Ted of all sorts of things.' Her eyes filled with pain. 'He even accused him of stealing.'

Charlotte was instantly thrown back to her conversation with Jett last night. She frowned at Ellen. 'He said something to me about some paintings.'

'That's right.' Ellen laughed bitterly. 'He's accusing Ted of stealing them. But he knows that's not true. They were sold to pay for repairs—and Ted has all the bills and receipts to prove it.'

She looked at Charlotte in despair. 'It's all a set-up. He just wants rid of us and is going to use any excuse to do it.'

That was precisely what had occurred to Charlotte earlier and now it appeared that she'd been right, she decided as she dropped Lucas off at his nursery group. And the whole situation was deeply shocking. The way Jett was behaving was utterly monstrous.

She had a flash of remembrance of that passionate embrace they'd shared—for there was no doubt about it, it had been passionate!—and instantly she felt her cheeks burn with shame.

How could she have done it? she wondered in bafflement. How could she have felt such a storm of desire for a man who stood against every decent thing she believed in?

Back at Penforth Manor, with all these questions still unanswered, Charlotte parked her old Renault in its usual corner of the courtyard, observing with dismay that Jett's Jaguar was still there. She didn't want to see him now. She still felt too confused. But perhaps he was in his study or out in the garden, and she could just sneak up to her room and stay out of his way.

She was just halfway across the hallway when these hopes fell apart.

'I have a message for you.' Suddenly Jett's voice spoke from behind her. 'Sara, your new recruit, just phoned.'

'Oh, yes?' Charlotte swung round with a start to face him, composing herself, draining all expression from her face, telling herself that last night had never happened. 'And what was the message?' she asked in a calm tone.

But a strange thing had happened as she looked into his face. Suddenly her heart, totally belying her cool expression, had broken into an excited jerky gallop. She felt a tingle go through her from her scalp to her toenails, and suddenly not only did last night feel very real again, but she could also understand perfectly why it had happened.

He's magic, she thought. Male magic personified. Every inch of him is raw, beautiful, sensuous manhood. Just to look into his face made her feel weak at the knees.

He was standing in the drawing-room doorway, leaning lightly against the door-jamb, hands thrust into his trouser pockets, the sleeves of his cream cotton shirt rolled back.

For a moment he surveyed her, his head tilted slightly. 'I'm afraid it's not good news,' he said.

Charlotte was still in the process of trying to rein in her racing heart. 'Oh?' she responded breathlessly. 'Then you'd better tell me what it is.'

'She won't be coming, after all.' Jett's expression was uncaring. Charlotte even thought she detected the hint of a callous smile. 'She says she won't be able to start until next week, after all.'

'That's very strange. She gave me her word.'
Looking into his face, Charlotte wondered if he was
lying—or worse, if he had set this up.

'Well, the situation's changed. Some family ob-
ligation. She said she's very sorry, but it can't be
helped.'

'I find this all very surprising.' Charlotte was over
her moment of madness. As she looked into Jett's
face now, all she felt was anger. 'She promised me
absolutely that she'd be able to start today.'

Jett shrugged. 'As I told you, the situation's
changed.'

'Perhaps I'd better phone and check.'

Charlotte was quivering with fury. He *had* set
this up. Suddenly, she was sure of it. But even as
she stepped, tight-lipped, towards the phone,
Annie, dustpan in hand, suddenly appeared from
the kitchen.

'She's terribly sorry, Miss Channing,' the girl told
her. 'But her grandmother's been taken poorly and
her mum's had to go and look after her—so Sara's
got to stay at home to look after her dad. He's got
a bad leg, you see, and finds it hard to get about.'

She paused and bit her lip apologetically. 'But
she said she'll definitely be able to start next week.'

'I see. Thank you, Annie.' Charlotte smiled at
the girl, who was already disappearing back into
the kitchen. And suddenly she was feeling a little
annoyed with herself for having so very nearly made
a scene.

What had got into her? Why did she suddenly
feel so vulnerable? It was this wretched man in front
her, turning her upside-down!

She turned back to face him, carefully gathering her poise about her. 'Well,' she said. 'This is really most unfortunate.'

'Yes, I thought you'd think that. It rather puts you on the spot. Especially now, with a guest coming to stay. Annie has already prepared the spare room and I have a lunch date, so there's no immediate problem for you...'

He paused and fixed her with a sharp blue look. 'However, there's the small matter of dinner this evening...'

Charlotte had already thought of that. It looked like *she* was going to have to cook it! What chance would there be of finding a cook at this late hour?

Still, fending off the inevitable, Charlotte tried a long shot. 'Couldn't you take your guest out for dinner?' she suggested.

'I could, but I don't plan to. I'd prefer to dine at home. My guest will be tired after her journey. I'm sure she won't feel like going out.'

'I see. In that case, I'll have to see what I can do.'

'I'd be grateful if you would.' Jett straightened slightly and drew a wad of crisp banknotes from his pocket. He held them out to her. 'This ought to more than cover it.'

As Charlotte stepped towards him to take the money, she could see at a glance that there was at least a hundred pounds there.

She flicked him an oblique look. 'What are you expecting? Caviare and cordon bleu? I think I ought to warn you that opening a can of spaghetti is just about the limit of my culinary skills.'

It had been a mistake to challenge him. Charlotte realised that instantly. As she reached out to take the money, his fingers closed around her wrist.

'Don't play games with me,' he growled at her. 'I don't like playing games.'

'I wasn't playing games.'

Charlotte blinked up into his face and felt herself go hot and cold all at once. The touch of him and his nearness were making her blood rush.

She gulped. 'Can I help it if I'm a lousy cook?'

'I don't believe you're a lousy cook. Not for one second.' He smiled a slow smile that made her blood rush even faster and, tightening his hold on her wrist, drew her even closer. 'From what I've seen, you're the type of girl who does everything well. Like I keep telling you, you're a girl of many talents.'

Charlotte knew she should be feeling outraged. How dared he bully her like this? But outrage was the one thing she wasn't feeling. In fact, as her gaze slid from his eyes to his mouth, to Charlotte's total dismay, she longed to kiss him.

Closing her eyes, she pleaded, 'But I'm no good in the kitchen.'

'I'll bet you are, when you put your mind to it. You'd be good at anything you put your mind to.'

To her absolute horror, with his free hand he reached up and brushed her mouth with the flat of his thumb. The sensations that shot through nailed her to the floor.

Charlotte opened her eyes then, aware that her lips had parted. Kiss me! Please kiss me! she was silently pleading.

He did not oblige immediately. For a moment he just gazed at her, but, very strongly, Charlotte could sense in him the same fire of intensity that was burning, quite out of control, within her.

And then, answering her prayers, he bent to capture her lips with his.

It was only a very brief kiss, but it felt like an explosion. As their lips met, the air all around them seemed to crackle.

Then it was over and he was drawing away and smiling down at her. 'You see. I told you so,' he said.

Charlotte was dimly aware that he had released her and that she was standing there holding the wad of banknotes in her hand. In a kind of blur she watched him as he told her,

'So, you see, knowing you and your many and varied talents, I shall expect a delicious three-course meal on the table tonight by eight o'clock.

'Don't worry about the wine,' he added. 'I'll see to that.'

But Charlotte hadn't waited to listen to that last part. She was fleeing across the hall and up the staircase, once again appalled at herself and how she had behaved.

There was only one way, Charlotte decided, to cope with what was happening to her, and that was to shut it right out of her mind and concentrate instead on the task before her.

She must forget about Jett and just think of tonight's dinner. Otherwise, there was a good chance she would end up going mad.

And, besides, tonight's dinner required her full concentration. The task before her was not a small one!

Charlotte had been exaggerating a little when she'd claimed she couldn't cook. She definitely didn't rate cooking as her top accomplishment, but she wasn't really a bad cook—when she had a cook-book to follow!

So, since there was not a cook-book to be found in the kitchen at the manor—Mrs Kibble had evidently used her own—the first thing she did after driving to the local village was head straight for the bookshop and buy a book on French cooking. She might as well aim high, she decided with a wry smile!

Then she sat in the next-door coffee-shop and pored over it for half an hour, picking out suitable recipes and making a list of ingredients, before driving to the supermarket and loading up with what she needed. She was exhausted by the time she went to pick up Lucas at twelve.

Fortunately, it was a sunny day, so after the two of them had had lunch Lucas was quite happy to play out in the garden. Charlotte sat in a corner, studying her cook-book, rehearsing step by step how she would go about her preparations. Oh, lord, she prayed, let's hope nothing goes wrong.

The first thing that went wrong, predictably, was Jett.

He was in the kitchen, making himself some coffee, when she arrived back at the manor just after five-thirty.

'My, that looks promising,' he observed with an amused smile as, studiously ignoring him, Charlotte dumped her shopping bags on the kitchen worktop and proceeded to empty them of their contents. 'Tell me what you're going to make with all that.'

Charlotte gritted her teeth. She didn't need this waste of time. 'Asparagus and ham salad, followed by veal cutlets *à la Normande* with sautéed courgettes and tomatoes,' she told him tightly. 'And for pudding I'm making little pots of vanilla cream.'

'Sounds good,' He set the percolator on the hob, then leaned against the kitchen table to watch her. 'I'm glad you decided against the canned spaghetti.'

'Don't bank on it. It could still come to that if all this doesn't turn out. Which could well happen,' she added irritably, 'if you insist on standing watching me for the next two hours!'

'You're right. I'd be better sitting.' With a flash of a wicked smile that was clearly designed to irritate her further, Jett pulled out a chair and proceeded to sit down. 'I won't get in your way. Just pretend I'm not here.'

She was already trying to do that, but it was easier said than done. With a snort of annoyance, Charlotte turned her back on him and proceeded to search for her bag of shallots. 'I'm not used to cooking in front of an audience,' she said sharply.

'Not even an audience of one?' She could tell he was still smiling. 'Surely you and your boyfriend cook together?'

'And what makes you think I have a boyfriend?' She'd found the bag of shallots and now was setting them in a pile with the other vegetables she'd need.

'What's the matter? Have you fallen out with him? I'm sorry to hear that. I got the impression, last time we met, that it was a pretty serious thing.'

What was he talking about? Charlotte turned to frown at him, at the same time rummaging for her new cook-book and turning to the pages she'd marked with bits of paper.

'What do you mean "last time we met"?' she demanded.

'You were writing him a letter. Don't you remember? You were so absorbed in it I seem to recall you forgot Uncle Oscar's injection.'

So, that was what he was on about! Charlotte was surprised he remembered that first encounter all those months ago. She glanced round to inform him, 'I wasn't writing to my boyfriend. I told you that at the time and it happens to be true. And I hadn't forgotten about your uncle's injection.'

'So, who were you writing to?'

'I wasn't writing to anyone. I was just writing. Scribbling. Nothing, really.'

She kept her eyes carefully averted as she told him this whopper. The truth was she'd been sketching out her first Bertie Rabbit story. But such secrets were secrets she'd never share with Jett Ashton. She'd come close once before, but never again!

To her relief, he wasn't interested in her secrets anyway. As she proceeded to search in the cupboards for pans, and the percolator on the hob began to bubble, he rose to his feet and poured himself a cup of coffee. Over his shoulder he asked her, 'Do you fancy a cup?'

'I don't have time for coffee. I'm really very busy.'

Charlotte threw him a look that invited him quite plainly just to take his cup of coffee and kindly leave.

No doubt that was what prompted him to do the very opposite. He picked up his coffee-cup and re-seated himself at the table. Then, addressing her angry back, he asked, 'So, tell me about the boyfriend.'

'What boyfriend?'

'Surely you have one?'

'And why must I have one? A girl can live without a boyfriend, you know.'

'But she can live better with one. Wouldn't you agree?'

'It depends on the boyfriend.'

'And what is that supposed to mean? Do I take it you've had some bad luck in the boyfriend department?'

Charlotte was trying to read the instructions in her cook-book at the same time as she was being forced to carry on this irritating conversation. She bent to search for a chopping board, but then paused and turned to Jett. Perhaps if she were to satisfy his impudent curiosity, he would shut up and leave her to get on with the job.

She said in the tone of someone trying to explain relativity to a five-year-old, 'I've had a couple of boyfriends. One was semi-serious. His name was Jim. We went out for a couple of years. But six months ago we decided the relationship was going nowhere, so we split up and went our separate ways with no hard feelings.'

And with that she turned back to continue her search for a chopping board.

'And there's been no one since?'

Charlotte gritted her teeth. 'No one worth mentioning. The occasional dinner date. But I can assure you I'm perfectly happy with things the way they are.'

She had managed to find a chopping board and now she was looking for a knife. 'Dice shallots finely', it said in the instructions. She found the knife drawer, grabbed one and started dicing.

'I'm sure you'd be even happier if things were different. For all of us life is better when we have a mate.'

For some reason, as he said that, Charlotte turned to look at him, feeling herself drown in the marvellous blue of his eyes and jolted by the terrible sadness that suddenly swept through her. What a tragedy it was that he was involved with Imelda.

Instantly, she was horrified. Where had such a shocking thought come from? A little shakily, biting her lip, she turned back to her dicing.

'I see you weren't joking.' Suddenly, Jett spoke again. 'You're certainly not very good at chopping onions.'

Charlotte felt a rush of annoyance, a rather welcome sensation, and turned round with a sharp look. 'You do it, then!'

Jett shook his head and smiled. 'I wouldn't dream of it. You're the cook. I wouldn't dream of butting in.'

'In that case, don't butt in!'

Once more Charlotte turned her back on him, feeling her annoyance with him quadruple. Though she had to admit to herself, as she glanced down at her chopping board, that he was right, she wasn't doing a very good job. Her finely diced shallots were more like chunks!

'You're using the wrong knife.' Jett was butting in again. And he was enjoying every minute of this. She could hear the smile in his voice. 'You can't expect to do the job right if you use the wrong knife.'

'And what sort of knife should I be using, since you seem to know so much about it?' Her knife poised in her hand, Charlotte shot him a look that told him precisely what she felt like doing with it. 'What's wrong with the one I happen to be using?'

'Nothing, but it's not a vegetable knife.' Jett leaned back in his chair, stretching out his legs and crossing them at the ankles. He wasn't even trying to keep the smile from his face.

Charlotte glanced at the offending knife. He was probably right, she thought irritably. The blade was a little on the short side. With a sigh she tossed it down, pulled open the knife drawer and rummaged inside it for a moment.

Then she held one up and enquired sarcastically. 'How about this one? Is this one any better?'

'Much better.' Jett nodded. 'Good girl,' he approved.

Good girl! Damned cheek! Charlotte turned back to her shallots, simultaneously irked and pleased to see that the new knife improved her handiwork enormously. And suddenly she was curious. Over her shoulder, she asked him, 'How come you know so much about knives?'

'Oh, it's just one of my countless areas of expertise.' He smiled for a moment at her angrily turned back. Then he drained his coffee-cup and told her, 'Actually, I worked as a cook for a while when I was a student.'

'You? A cook?' Charlotte turned then to look at him. 'Where?' she demanded, not sure if she believed him.

'In a big hotel in Chicago. I was a short-order cook.'

'But why?' Charlotte frowned. Suddenly, she was bewildered. 'Why on earth were you working as a cook?'

'To earn a few dollars. Certainly not for the love of it.' Jett threw her a quick smile. 'Though I quite enjoyed it, in a way. I made a couple of very good friends.'

Charlotte regarded him from beneath her lashes for a moment. Jett Ashton having to work in order to earn a few dollars? This didn't sound at all like the picture she'd been painted. She'd been led to believe he'd always had things easy. That he'd been born with the proverbial silver spoon in his mouth.

And that obviously wasn't so. Suddenly, she was curious.

'How about you?' It seemed he was curious, too. 'Did you have to do odd jobs, too, when you were a student?'

'I did a few when I was still at school. I once worked as a waitress.' She laughed as she turned back to get on with her dicing. 'So, although I'm not so good at dicing shallots, I'm pretty good at carrying half a dozen things at once. A skill that came in pretty useful when I was on the wards.'

'Yes, you said you'd been a ward nurse.' Jett rose from his chair and came to stand alongside her, leaning his hips against the worktop. 'So, what made you go into nursing in the first place?'

'Partly my parents' influence. Both of them are nurses.' Charlotte smiled a fond smile. 'And so is my sister. There's a bit of nursing tradition in our family.'

'Are they all private, too?'

'No, they all work in the Health Service. I'm the only one who opted out.'

'And what made you do that?'

'Partly lack of money.' Charlotte dropped her gaze. 'Although it wasn't just that.'

'And what other reasons were there?'

As he cast another curious glance at her, just for a moment Charlotte hesitated. Then she said, 'Private nursing gives me more free time.'

'Free time to do what?'

Again she hesitated. Her secret ambition was known to only a few—her family who all backed her one hundred and one per cent and a couple of her oldest, closest friends. And though she felt tempted to confide in him, just as she had once before, at the same time she feared it would probably not be wise to add Jett to her list of trusted confidantes.

But then suddenly he smiled and answered his own question. 'I know,' he told her. 'You need free time to do your painting and write up those stories you're so good at telling in your notebook.' He winked at her. 'I knew you were up to something!'

As she blushed, he settled himself more comfortably against the worktop. 'Come on,' he urged her. 'I'm fascinated. Tell me all about it.'

To her amazement, Charlotte did and she found confiding in him easy.

'I think it's great,' he encouraged her. 'We should all follow our dreams. And, as I've told you from the beginning, you've definitely got talent. I have absolutely no doubt at all that you'll make it.'

The time simply sped by as she chatted away to him, telling him how it had all started with those stories in the children's ward and how it had gradually developed over the past couple of years to the point where she was now on the brink of publishing her stories.

And it was a joy to be telling him. He seemed so interested. There was no sign at all of the abrasive Jett Ashton that she had once believed him to be. This man she was talking to definitely had heart!

And in spite of all the chatter, the job in hand got done. An hour later she'd made unbelievable progress. The veal cutlets were simmering in a pan on the hob, the dessert was prepared and cooling in the fridge and the courgettes and tomatoes were all ready to be sautéed.

'I can't believe it!' Charlotte smiled with satisfaction. 'All that's left to be done is lay the table, uncork the wine and slice some bread.' She really had been incredibly efficient!

'I'll look after the wine, so don't worry about that. I've put a bottle in the fridge. More than enough for one. Imelda won't be drinking any.'

That mention of Imelda caused a dull thud inside Charlotte. Instantly, she felt all her happiness drain out of her. In the intimacy of the past hour she'd forgotten about Imelda.

To hide her suddenly pale cheeks, she turned away quickly and pretended to check the progress of the veal cutlets. Get a grip on yourself, she told herself sharply.

Jett was unaware of her reaction. 'As a matter of fact,' he was saying, 'it's time I was on my way to the station. Her train gets in in half an hour.'

He turned to smile at Charlotte. 'I hope her train's not late. I'm starving and everything smells delicious!'

But then, as she made no response, he paused and frowned at her. He touched her arm. 'What's up?' he asked.

Sick with humiliation, Charlotte kept her back turned. What had got into her? She was making a complete fool of herself. 'Nothing,' she replied. But she had failed to convince him. Very gently, Jett was turning her round to face him.

He touched her cheek with his finger. 'Look,' he told her softly, 'there's no time to go into details at the moment, but you can take my word for it there's nothing between Imelda and me. As I told you, that's over. Strictly past tense.'

'Then why does she keep phoning you?'

'I can't stop her phoning.'

'And why have you invited her to stay at your home?'

'She invited herself.'

'But you could have turned her down. You could have told her not to come.'

Charlotte could scarcely believe she was actually saying these things. She must sound like a jealous wife giving her husband the third degree! She half expected Jett to tell her to mind her own business.

And to be honest, she wouldn't have blamed him if he had.

But he did not. Instead, he told her, his blue eyes serious, 'Look, I can assure you it's definitely over. But Imelda's got a problem. That's why she keeps phoning. She wants my help to sort it out.'

'And that's all?'

'That's all. Imelda's the past. Like your Jim.' He bent and kissed the tip of her nose. 'And now will you let me go to the station?'

Charlotte smiled back at him, feeling foolish but happy. She nodded. 'Yes, of course. You don't want to be late.'

'You're smiling again. That's what I like to see.' He held her for a moment and, as he released her, Charlotte could feel the reluctance in him. 'But I really have to go. I'll see you later.'

Charlotte watched him leave, aware of a sudden glow about her. Something had happened between them. Something special. It was crazy, but she was tingling from her toes to her scalp.

And Imelda was no threat. Jett had made that very clear. He was helping her, that was all, perhaps with some financial problem or some joint business they'd been involved in. Whatever it was, it was nothing personal.

In no time at all, her remaining chores were done. Through in the dining-room, humming happily to herself, Charlotte put the finishing touches to the table and cast a quick glance round the room. Everything looked in order. Then she noticed the curtains. One of them had been pulled back a little further than the other.

Still humming happily, she crossed to the window to adjust it and instantly fell silent, freezing in her tracks.

She hadn't heard the car draw up, but there it stood out on the driveway. And, standing right beside it, were Jett and Imelda.

Charlotte stared numbly at the scene, very still, scarcely breathing, her stomach suddenly as heavy as a bucket of wet cement.

What was it he had said to her less than an hour ago? 'There's nothing between Imelda and me. As I told you, that's over. Strictly past tense'.

Well, the past, it would appear, had suddenly become the present, for there was definitely something going on between them now. They were standing with their arms wrapped round one another.

You snake! Charlotte thought helplessly, feeling her heart crack inside her. You dirty, lying, cheating snake!

CHAPTER SIX

THE front door opened as Charlotte was halfway across the hall, heading from the dining-room back to the kitchen. And in walked Jett, as brazen as three brass monkeys, looking as though butter wouldn't melt in his mouth.

'You're back already?'

Charlotte was justly proud of the surprise she managed to inject in her voice. Jett had no idea she'd witnessed that performance in the driveway.

'Let me introduce you to Imelda.' He turned with a light smile to the voluptuously striking dark-haired girl who had followed him through the door and who stood now at his side. 'Imelda, this is Charlotte. Charlotte, Imelda.'

Imelda barely moved a muscle. She certainly didn't step forward and she didn't even bother to hold out her hand. No wonder, Charlotte thought; in that tight dress she's wearing, any physical movement is bound to be a little tricky.

That was bitchy, she reproved herself, instantly guilty. Jett's the one you're mad at, remember, not Imelda.

But a moment later she was feeling much less guilty as Imelda twined both hands around Jett's arm and looked coldly into Charlotte's face. 'Who are you?' she demanded. 'Are you the domestic?'

'Yes, I suppose you could say that—at least for the moment.' Charlotte looked into the girl's face

101

with its haughty brown eyes, sulky little mouth and disdainful expression. This one really thinks she's something, she thought.

'No, Charlotte's not the domestic.' Jett had intervened. He looked down with an indulgent smile at Imelda. 'Actually, she's a nurse, but she's helping me out for the moment. It's a long story. I'll tell you all about it later.'

Imelda shrugged her slim shoulders, clearly not the least bit interested. Then she tossed another disdainful glance at Charlotte and indicated her suitcase, which Jett had dropped by the front door. 'Perhaps you wouldn't mind taking my case up to my room,' she drawled. Then she fluttered a glance at Jett. 'When's dinner, darling?'

'In about half an hour's time.' Jett smiled another indulgent smile. Then he flicked a quick glance in Charlotte's direction before steering Imelda off towards the drawing-room. 'Don't worry, I'll deal with the case,' he told her.

Too right you will! Charlotte was quietly fuming as she turned on her heel and headed back to the kitchen. Who did that wretched female think she was? 'Are you the domestic?' What a damned impudent cheek!

Back in the kitchen, she seized a spatula and stirred furiously at the courgettes. Then she grabbed a loaf of bread and started slicing it savagely. And as for Jett—the lying, cheating snake!

She was still slicing when he appeared, alone, in the kitchen doorway.

'Everything OK? Will dinner be ready on time?'

Charlotte did not glance up, but continued with her slicing. 'Don't worry,' she responded sharply.

'Everything's under control. Dinner will be on the table by eight.'

'Good.'

He was still standing there. From the corner of her eye Charlotte could see the toes of his shoes pointing towards her. And she could sense he was smiling an amused smile as he added, 'You're going to cut right through that breadboard if you're not careful.'

He was right. She was taking her anger out on the bread. Charlotte stopped her violent slicing and raised her eyes to look at him, wishing she could summon the poise to come straight out and tell him what an unprincipled liar she thought he was.

But she didn't trust herself to do it without revealing her own emotions. Her voice would break. She'd end up looking an idiot.

So, instead she said tightly, 'I'm sorry about the breadboard. I really ought to know better... as the domestic.'

'Imelda didn't mean anything by that remark.' Jett raised one dark eyebrow as he answered. He seemed surprised by the harsh, abrasive note in her voice. 'I wouldn't think twice about it,' he added.

'Don't worry, I won't.' Charlotte was clutching the breadknife tightly, her knuckles as bone-white as the livid spots on her cheeks. And then she heard herself asking, 'Just how long will she be staying?'

'Just as long as she cares to. Why do you ask?'

As he spoke, his tone had developed a distinct edge.

But Charlotte ignored the warning. 'I was just wondering,' she flared at him, 'how long I'm going to have to endure the pleasure of her company.'

She was doing this all wrong. She knew that as the words gushed out of her. It was Jett she was mad at, not Imelda, so why was she saying all these silly, spiteful things?

Jett delivered her a hard look. 'What the devil's got into you? If you don't mind my saying so you're behaving like a spoilt child.'

Well, she'd had that coming—but still his sharpness wounded her. Charlotte dropped her gaze abruptly to hide the sudden tears that burned like hot pokers at the backs of her eyes.

She stared down at the abused breadboard and suddenly longed to strike back at him. 'What are you standing there for?' she demanded, her tone sarcastic. 'Why don't you do something useful, like taking your girlfriend's suitcase up to her room—instead of wasting time bandying words with the domestic? I'm sure she wouldn't approve of that at all!' she added brittly.

A dark look crossed Jett's eyes. He reached out and caught her arm. 'Let's get things straight, right from the start!' he growled.

Taken by surprise, Charlotte's heart had leapt within her at the sudden cool touch of his flesh against hers. As she tried to snatch her arm free, her pulse was suddenly racing. 'Get your hands off me!' she squeaked. 'What the devil do you think you're doing?'

'Putting you straight.' He gave her a small shake, then twisted her round sharply so that she was facing him fully. 'I suggest you get all of this hostility out of your system right now. Whatever you may think of Imelda, kindly keep it to yourself. While she's here I shall expect you to treat her as you'd treat any other guest—with respect and politeness and consideration...'

He smiled a grim smile. 'Do I make myself clear?'

'Oh, perfectly clear.' Charlotte was hating him at that moment, more than she had ever hated anyone in her life. 'Perhaps you'd like me to curtsy every time I address her and crawl backwards on all fours whenever I leave the room?'

'What a quaint idea.' Jett tilted his head and smiled at her. And the pain that drove through her in that instant was quite shocking. It was unbearable to think he belonged to Imelda.

He continued to smile down at her. 'But such extremes won't be called for. Just everyday politeness will be quite sufficient.'

Then he narrowed his eyes and seemed about to add something, but at the last minute thought better of it and told her instead,

'So, just bear that in mind.' His tone had become gritty again. 'On no account must Imelda be upset. If you have any complaints, bring them to me.'

'I'm sure I'll have no complaints.'

Charlotte regarded him bitterly. If she did, she would keep them to herself. He'd have better things to do then listen to her gripes. She thought again of the scene she had witnessed through the window and felt a rush of anger and foolish jealousy tear through her. What an unspeakable two-faced liar he was.

The next couple of hours were something of an ordeal. As Charlotte ferried the various courses between kitchen and dining-room, she was praying for this wretched evening to end. Just the sight of Jett and Imelda seated together at the table was like a fist in the midriff each time she walked into the room.

And yet, she couldn't help thinking, as she brought them their main course, the atmosphere between them was not all sweetness and light.

It was true that every time Charlotte walked into the room their heads would be together, engrossed in some intimate conversation, which ceased the moment they became aware of her presence. And it was true, too, that Imelda seemed unable to keep her hands off Jett, constantly caressing his fingers or stroking his arm. But, increasingly, Charlotte was aware of a tension between them.

Jett seemed to be enduring, rather than enjoying Imelda's caresses, and there was a frown between his brows that had barely lifted all evening. And suddenly, belatedly, Charlotte understood.

When Jett had said the romance was over he'd meant it was over for him. Imelda, it would appear, had other ideas. Hence the battery of phone calls and her pursuit of him to the manor. She was desperately trying to win him back.

She felt a small flicker of sympathy and a slightly larger one of hope. Not on any account would she ever wish anyone heartache, but personally she'd much prefer it if Jett were unattached.

And the odds were in her favour, she couldn't help thinking, for somehow she couldn't see Jett being won over. If he'd made up his mind it was over, then it was.

Charlotte was feeling a great deal more light-hearted as she cleared away the dessert things, piling them carefully on to her tray, and paused to enquire, 'Will you both be having coffee?'

Jett glanced up at her. 'Yes, I think so.' Then he tossed her a warm smile. 'That really was a first-class meal.'

Charlotte felt her heart swell. 'Thank you,' she told him. It was flattering that the first real smile he'd smiled all evening had been directed so spontaneously at her. She smiled back at him. 'I'm very glad you enjoyed it.'

Jett had turned now to address Imelda. 'Do you feel like coffee, dear?'

Dear.

The word was like a skewer thrust into Charlotte's heart. Her fingers that held the tray tightened a little. But she took comfort in the observation that it had been said with little feeling. The way one might address a child one barely knew.

There was a pause as Imelda considered her answer. Then she shook her head. 'No, I don't think so. Ask her if I can have a cup of weak tea.'

Jett turned back to Charlotte. 'You heard,' he told her. 'One strong black coffee and one weak tea.'

'Tell her to make sure it's really very weak. And it has to be Lapsang Souchong. I won't drink anything else.'

Jett repeated the instruction. 'Lapsang Souchong. Very weak.'

Charlotte was finding it hard not to glare at Imelda. Did she have to relay every message through Jett? Perhaps she considered it beneath her dignity to communicate directly with the domestic? As she turned on her heel and headed back to the kitchen, she was seething fit to burst at the seams.

Back in the kitchen she dumped the tray on the table, laid the percolator on the hob and filled the kettle with water. What an impossible female! How could Jett ever have stood her? She had no manners and she couldn't even order a cup of tea for herself!

But he did stand her, even now, when he clearly wanted the affair over. He was patient with her and indulgent and endlessly polite. He'd made it very clear to Charlotte that Imelda mustn't be upset.

And Charlotte couldn't make up her mind how his attitude made her feel. Should she feel glad to discover that he was capable of such kindness, or sorry that in this case he wasn't being a little more ruthless?

Jett's coffee was nearly ready and the kettle was boiling when, a couple of minutes later, Jett appeared in the kitchen doorway. Charlotte glanced up at him with a start, feeling that same helpless flutter that she never failed to feel whenever she looked into his face.

'It'll be ready in a minute,' she said. 'I'm just about to bring it through.'

As she was speaking, he had crossed to the kitchen table and stood watching her as she laid cups and things on a tray. 'It's OK,' he said. 'You don't have to bother. Imelda's gone up to her room. I'll take her tea up.'

'I can take it up.'

'No need. I'll do it.' He smiled. 'You've already done enough this evening.'

'It would be no trouble.'

She hated to insist. She felt sure her motives must be patently obvious. For the truth was just the thought of Jett going to Imelda's room made her skin turn to ice all over. In the privacy of her own room, Imelda would be all over him, and how would a red-blooded man like Jett be able to resist? Imelda, after all, was a beautiful girl.

But as she reached for the boiling kettle and poured some water into a small teapot, Jett was equally insistent.

'I wouldn't dream of asking you to do that,' he told her. 'No, I'll take it up to her. I assure you it's no problem.'

'What about your coffee?' Charlotte kept her eyes on what she was doing as she swirled the water round in the pot, then emptied it out and spooned in a tiny measure of Lapsang Souchong. As she poured hot water over it, she enquired in a carefully casual tone, 'Do you want me to serve you your coffee in the dining-room when you've finished delivering Imelda's tea?'

She held her breath as she waited for his answer. It was ridiculous, but she felt so tight she could scarcely breathe.

'No need for that. I'll take the coffee with me. Just put the whole lot on a tray.'

It was the answer she'd feared, but it was also the one she'd half expected. Suddenly she could barely see what she was doing for the hurt and anger that were spiralling inside her.

And then Jett did the unforgivable. He reached out and touched her. 'I wasn't joking when I said that was a first-class meal. You really excelled yourself, you know.'

'I could say the same for you!'

It was out before she could stop it. Charlotte's grey eyes flashed as she snatched her arm away, and she felt deeply gratified by the surprised look on his face.

'And what is that supposed to mean?' he said.

'I think you know what it means! It means you're a liar! A rotten liar who just uses women! It's obvious you don't give a damn about Imelda, yet you're quite prepared to take advantage of her feelings for you.'

'Take advantage?' He had quite recovered from his surprise and his tone now was level, if a little sharp. 'What makes you think I have any plans to take advantage?'

'Oh, excuse me! I forgot!' His calmness was infuriating. 'You're not taking advantage, you're just helping her, aren't you? That's the story we're supposed to swallow!'

Charlotte was shaking with fury. Hadn't he taken advantage of her as well? Hadn't he pretended to feel something when he clearly felt nothing?

'You're a liar!' she accused him. 'A womanising liar! Everything Ellen and Ted ever said about you is true!'

Jett's expression changed then. A hard look touched his eyes. 'So, you've been listening to Ted and Ellen again. In that case, no wonder your brain's got all twisted.'

'My brain twisted? You're the one whose brain is twisted!' As she spoke, Charlotte was shifting the things around on the tray. She felt like picking the whole lot up and chucking it at him. 'Your brain's so twisted you don't even know what the truth is!'

She thrust the tray at him. 'There! It's ready. You can go up to Imelda now and continue your therapy.'

'Thank you. I will.' Calmly, he took the tray, though his eyes were as black as thunder in his face. Then he headed for the door, pausing only to advise her, 'When we've finished I'll leave the tray outside the bedroom door. Feel free to come and pick it up whenever you wish.'

Charlotte watched him go, her whole body trembling. I hate him, she kept telling herself over and over. He's a worthless, rotten, cynical liar and I wouldn't have him if he offered himself to me on a plate!

But no matter how often nor how angrily she repeated it the gnawing pain inside her just refused to go away.

After switching on the dishwasher, Charlotte went up to her room just a matter of a few minutes after Jett had left.

It wasn't that she intended spying on him, she solemnly assured herself—though Imelda's room was just two doors from her own, which put her in a perfect position to monitor his comings and goings!

And, indeed, she had barely closed the door behind her when she heard Imelda's door open and Jett's voice saying, 'Goodnight.'

Charlotte froze where she stood in the middle of the room and listened to his footsteps recede down the corridor. So, nothing had happened, she thought, her heart lightening, feeling a flood of mingled relief and shame. Jett had not, after all, taken advantage of Imelda. It would appear he'd simply drunk his coffee and left.

She sank down on to the bed with a sigh of exhaustion. I'm driving myself crazy, she told herself sternly. That outburst downstairs was nothing less than a disgrace. I'll finish in the madhouse if I keep this up!

And for what? For Jett? That would indeed be madness. Jett wasn't for her. She had always known that. And right now he had enough on his plate with Imelda. No, the best thing she could do was put Jett out of her mind.

She tried. As she climbed beneath the covers a little later, Charlotte struggled to think of anything but Jett. She thought of Lucas. She thought about her painting. She thought about her parents. She seized at anything and everything she could.

But in the end it was no good. It was Jett's face that stood before her, his scent that hung deliciously in her nostrils and the memory of the touch of him that warmed her skin beneath the covers as at long last she drifted off to sleep.

Next morning, after she'd dropped Lucas off at his nursery group, Charlotte went into town to do a bit of window shopping. Then, when it grew too warm, she sat for a while in the park and read the newspaper she'd bought from cover to cover.

For the most part she'd got over her madness of last night and was actually managing not to think of Jett all the time. Though it was best to stay away from the manor for the moment. She had no desire to spend the morning tripping over Jett and Imelda.

And if they got hungry, they could darned well cook their own lunch!

She picked Lucas up at twelve as usual and they went back to the Coach House for a cheese-salad lunch. As they finished it off, Charlotte asked the little boy, 'How would you fancy going up to the manor this afternoon?'

Lucas's big brown eyes grew round. 'Ooh, yes, I'd like that. Maybe Uncle Jett will let me sail my boat on the lake.'

'I'm sure he will.'

Charlotte smiled to herself, pleased. Among the thoughts she'd busied herself with that morning had been thoughts of Ellen and Ted and the threat that hung over them that lately she seemed rather shamefully to have forgotten. And to redeem herself she'd worked out a plan that might save them— and step one of that plan required a visit to the manor.

As soon as the washing up was done, she and Lucas set off.

The first thing Charlotte saw as they came round the side of the big house, following the paved path that led to the rear gardens, was Imelda, wearing a skimpy fuchsia bikini, stretched out lazily on a sunbed.

No doubt this display was for Jett's benefit, she thought sourly, suddenly wishing she was wearing something a little more glamorous than a simple floral skirt and white cotton top!

'Welcome back!'

Next instant her heart leapt inside her, as, apparently from nowhere, Jett appeared before them, dressed in light trousers and a pale blue T-shirt and smiling down at Lucas as he spoke.

And this time at the sight of him, the child responded with a grin. 'Hello, Uncle Jett. Can I sail my boat on your lake?'

'Of course you can.' Jett was crouching down beside him, admiring the bright red yacht the child held in his hand. 'My, that's a splendid yacht. Let's see how well it goes.'

He glanced up at Charlotte. 'Are you coming to join us?'

His tone was equable, with not a hint of reproach. It seemed he had forgotten about her outburst last night. Or had enough sensitivity not to upbraid her in front of Lucas!

'No, if you don't mind, I'll leave you two together.' Charlotte smiled, relieved that there was to be no ugly scene and pleased that her plan was going so smoothly already. 'I'll just watch you from the patio.'

'Please yourself.' Jett was reaching for the child's hand. 'Come on, Lucas. Let's go find that lake.'

On the patio Charlotte seated herself on one of the white-painted chairs from where she had a perfect view of the lake. On her way there she'd directed a polite hello at Imelda, but there'd been no response, so she'd simply shrugged. Right now, Imelda wasn't what was on her mind. What was on her mind was Jett and Lucas.

And from what she could see, her plan was going perfectly. The two of them appeared to be getting on like a house on fire.

It was about half an hour later that, leaving Lucas with the gardener, who for the past five minutes had been joining in their game, Jett was suddenly heading back towards the house.

As he approached the patio, Charlotte rose to her feet. 'Is anything the matter? Is your game over? Do you want me to go and fetch Lucas back?'

Jett paused right in front of her and there was a glint in his eyes. 'No, our game's not over. I've just got to make a quick phone call.' Then he smiled and let his eyes trail slowly over her. 'But, talking of games, I know what your game is.'

Charlotte felt herself flush at the way he was looking at her. 'I don't know what you mean. What game?' she stuttered.

'You're a smart girl, I'll say that.' His head tilted to one side as he continued to let his eyes drift over her. 'You're trying to win me over. That's why you threw Lucas and me together. To try and soften my heart and save Ted and Ellen.' He reached out and touched her cheek. 'Isn't that so?'

He was dead on target. That was precisely what she'd been doing!

Charlotte gulped drily. 'I just thought you'd enjoy spending some time with Lucas.'

'And I do. Very much. I have to thank you. All the same...' He paused again and tilted her chin to look at him. 'All the same, don't you think that was just a little bit sneaky of you?'

Charlotte was finding it very hard to know what she was thinking. Suddenly her skin was burning where he was touching her and her soul seemed to be drowning in the sapphire pools of his eyes.

She opened her mouth, but no sound came out.

He had taken a step towards her. She saw his lips move. 'Do you know what I do to girls who do sneaky things like that?'

And then, before she had time to answer, he had propelled her behind a potted bay tree and was drawing her into his arms and kissing her.

Flames were leaping from her hair. Charlotte could feel them. And a tidal wave of sheer exhilaration was rushing through her. She sank into his arms, her lips parting in welcome, and felt the ground beneath her tremble.

But an instant later they were interrupted.

It was poor Annie, quite beetroot-coloured in her embarrassment. 'Come quickly,' she was saying. 'Miss Imelda's been taken ill.'

CHAPTER SEVEN

'WHAT'S wrong with her?'

Jett had released his hold on Charlotte instantly and had swung round to face the still beetroot-faced Annie.

'She's fainted, sir. Just like that. She got up from her sunbed and just fell in a heap. I think maybe she's had too much sun,' the girl added.

'Go and fetch a glass of water. I'll take her inside.'

Even as he spoke, Jett was heading across the garden to where Imelda still lay, as pale as a corpse, on the grass. And as Charlotte followed closely in his footsteps, mingled with the concern she felt for Imelda was a sense of grudging admiration for Jett.

He hadn't turned a hair when Annie had interrupted them in the full flow of that shamelessly passionate embrace. Charlotte, on the other hand, had turned as crimson as Annie. One thing you had to admit—the man was cool.

Imelda was already stirring when Jett and Charlotte reached her, shaking her head and blinking dopily.

'What happened? I must have passed out. Oh, lord, how silly of me.' She closed her eyes and sighed. 'I'm sorry, Jett.'

'How do you feel now?' As Jett began to scoop her up, Charlotte automatically reached out to take the girl's pulse and lay a hand against her forehead, testing for fever.

But Jett was having none of it. He began to move away, obliging Charlotte to drop her hands away. 'I'm taking her inside. She's had too much sun. She needs to lie down for a while.'

'You're probably right, but at least, let me take a look at her. After all, I am a qualified nurse!' Indignantly, Charlotte started to follow him.

'You're here to look after Lucas.' Jett nodded towards the child who, full of curiosity, was running towards them. 'So just you look after your business and I'll look after mine.' And with that he strode away from her across the grass.

Charlotte watched him go, debating whether she should follow. But to be honest she was pretty sure there was nothing serious wrong with Imelda. There'd been no sign of a fever and, in spite of her pallor, she seemed to have recovered more or less completely.

Perhaps she'd skipped lunch or maybe she was having her period or was just generally feeling a bit under the weather. And as Jett had said, too much sun probably hadn't helped.

So she let Jett go and turned to Lucas. 'Come on. Let's go to the patio and you can play with your train set.'

It was about ten minutes later when Jett reappeared. Charlotte was suddenly aware of him standing by her chair.

She looked up into his face, hating the way her heart turned over. 'How is Imelda now?' she wanted to know.

'She's fine.' He was lowering himself into one of the chairs beside her. 'I've advised her to lie down and have a rest for a while.'

'You're sure you don't want me to take a look at her?'

'No, that won't be necessary.' Jett shook his head. 'All she needs is a bit of a rest.'

Charlotte watched him for a moment beneath her lashes. His tone was an odd mixture of irritation and concern, as though he could gladly have done without this little upset and was only putting up with it because it was the decent thing to do. Then she remembered what Imelda had said as she'd lain there prostrate on the grass.

She'd said, 'I'm sorry, Jett'. And it had sounded so pathetic. She clearly knew that to Jett she was nothing but a nuisance and felt so vulnerable and insecure she even had to apologise for fainting. It was tragic. She must love Jett very much.

That realisation was oddly distressing. Suddenly Imelda wasn't just a pushy, bad-mannered girl any more. She was—what? Charlotte stopped herself in mid-sentence. She'd been about to add 'someone I can identify with'. And that, she told herself swiftly, was nonsense.

Sheer, utter nonsense, she emphasised mentally and turned disapprovingly to glance at Jett again.

'If it happens again, I shall insist on looking at her,' she told him. 'Either that or I shall call in a doctor. People don't keep fainting for no reason.'

'She doesn't keep fainting. It's only happened once.'

'Even so.'

'So just forget about it, will you?'

His tone was sharp. He'd had enough of the subject.

Then he narrowed his eyes at her, his expression sceptical. 'I must say I'm just a little surprised by this sudden display of concern from you.'

A blush touched Charlotte's cheeks. She couldn't argue with his suggestion that she wasn't particularly partial to Imelda. But right now, apart from her quite genuine concern, she was also feeling a little guilty.

Perhaps Imelda had fainted because she'd spotted her and Jett, locked in a clinch behind the potted bay tree. She'd leapt from her sunbed in a state of high emotion, then it had all been too much for her and she'd simply passed out.

But Charlotte had no wish to discuss that particular theory with Jett. Just thinking about that kiss had made her insides feel all funny.

She sketched a shrug with her shoulders. 'It's just natural human concern. Though, I admit, it's more than you appear to be feeling.'

'Would you prefer it if I cared more?' He tossed a lazy smile across at her. 'Are you saying I should be upstairs, glued to her bedside?'

Charlotte blushed scarlet. 'No. Not exactly.'

Jett continued to smile at her, leaning back in his chair, his bright blue eyes trailing impudently over her.

'I thought not,' he agreed. 'Certainly, last night you didn't seem too keen to have me hanging about her bedside.'

Poor Charlotte felt quite mortified. She stared at the patio floor tiles, wishing she could slip through the cracks in between. Did he really have to bring up the subject of last night?

But not only had he brought it up, he was refusing to drop it.

'But you needn't have worried,' he told her in that teasing tone. 'I just delivered the pot of tea and left.'

Charlotte almost said, 'I know.' But, luckily, she stopped herself. She had no wish for him to know she'd been monitoring his movements!

'So, you see,' he carried on, 'I really didn't have time to take advantage of Imelda, as you seemed to think was my intention.'

It was growing worse by the minute. Inwardly, Charlotte cringed. How could she have said all those things to him last night?

There was a moment of silence. Charlotte felt him lean towards her and sensed he was waiting for her to look up into his face. And she couldn't keep staring down at the floor indefinitely. Sooner or later, she was going to have to meet his gaze. She took a deep breath and raised her head slowly, steeling herself against the amusement she knew she would see in his face.

But there was no amusement there. His expression had grown serious.

As her eyes locked with his, he told her in a gentle tone, 'But, really, you ought to have known that anyway. I'd already told you how things stand between Imelda and me.'

As he said it, he reached out and took hold of her hand.

Charlotte felt her breath catch. A rush of pleasure went through her. His hand felt so deliciously strong against her own.

But in spite of these giddy feelings, she had to say what she was thinking. 'You told me how things stand from your point of view,' she told him. 'But what about from Imelda's? She still seems rather attached.'

She had thought he might take his hand away, but instead he did the opposite. Making her shiver, he laced his fingers with hers.

'That's not true.' He shook his head and looked deep into her eyes, making her poor stomach curl up and disappear. 'She's not attached. She's just feeling a little vulnerable. As I told you, she's got a bit of a problem at the moment, and I'm trying to help her sort it out.'

Jett sighed, letting his fingers twine lightly with hers. 'But let's not start going over all that again. Just take my word for it. We're not romantically involved.'

Charlotte wanted to believe him. More than anything. She looked down at his hand, his skin so dark against her own, and found herself wishing they could stay like this forever. But though she longed to drop the subject of Imelda, she had to ask him,

'What kind of a problem is she having?'

He paused just an instant before replying. As Charlotte glanced up, she thought she saw a sudden shadow touch his eyes.

Then he smiled and it was gone. 'It's rather personal,' he told her. 'I don't think Imelda would wish me to discuss it.'

Then he shook his head. 'Look, let's forget about Imelda. More than likely she'll be leaving to-morrow, anyway.'

He paused and held her eyes and raised her fingers to his lips and very, very softly kissed her fingertips. 'And then, at last, there'll be just you and me again and we can finally start getting to know each other a little better.'

The blue eyes seemed to swallow her. 'I think it's time we did, don't you?'

Charlotte really wasn't sure what she wanted to answer. That gently grazing kiss had electrified her fingertips and sent her brain into a kind of mental tailspin. She was almost relieved when a little voice piped up at her elbow,

'Charlotte, can I go to the lake and play with my boat again?'

'Of course you can.' Jett was rising to his feet instantly, tossing Charlotte a wryly amused smile as he did so. 'Let's all go,' he said. Then he held out his hand to Lucas. 'Come on. Let's show Charlotte how well you can handle that boat of yours.'

Charlotte rose to her feet, still feeling a little giddy. And as she followed Jett and Lucas across the garden to the lake edge she found herself looking at Jett's broad back and thinking, If I'm not very careful I could fall in love with this man.

Instantly, a warning bell rang in her head. In that case, be very, very careful! it said.

But by the end of the afternoon she knew that being careful wasn't going to be easy. Watching Jett play with Lucas simply knocked her defences lower.

He had endless patience with the child and a wonderful sense of fun that Charlotte hadn't really been aware of before. Either he was an exceedingly good actor or else he was enjoying himself every bit as much as Lucas and herself.

'Thank you,' she told him when it was time for Lucas and her to leave. 'That was a lovely afternoon. It was really very good of you.'

'It's me who should be thanking you for bringing Lucas here.' Jett tousled the child's hair and, smiling, winked down at him. 'I hope to see you back here very soon.'

'Oh, yes, please!' Lucas's eyes were shining. Then he glanced beseechingly at Charlotte. 'Can we really come back soon?'

'Of course we can.'

'You can come back whenever you like.' Jett bent down quickly to kiss the child's head. 'And the sooner the better, as far as I'm concerned.'

He accompanied them along the paved path that led to the front of the house and took Charlotte aside as they were saying their farewells.

'I'm taking Imelda out to dinner tonight—in order to save you having to cook,' he added quickly as a look touched her eyes. 'I'd invite you to join us, but it might be a bit awkward.' He winked at her. 'It's better if you just get on with some painting.'

Then he reached out and touched her cheek. 'But let's have dinner tomorrow. Just the two of us. Imelda should be gone by then.'

Charlotte nodded, delighted. 'OK,' she said.

A couple of minutes later, as she and Lucas headed down the driveway, Charlotte felt as though she was walking on air. What an unexpectedly wonderful day it had been!

She glanced down at Lucas with a sense of total confidence. Her little ploy had worked, of that she was now certain. For there was no doubt in her mind that a bond had now been forged between the child and his once hostile and distant second cousin.

Jett had become fond of the little boy. She had seen it in his eyes today. There'd been a genuine sense of closeness and caring.

She smiled to herself. So now Lucas was safe. And not only Lucas, but also Ted and Ellen. Jett would never have the heart to evict them now.

That on its own might almost have been enough to account for her bright smile and the new spring in her step. But the sparkle in her grey eyes had another cause entirely. Tomorrow, she and Jett were going to have dinner together!

At the very thought the ground seemed to bounce beneath her feet, so that with each step she took she was floating higher and higher.

And perhaps it was vertigo—though more probably not!—but her stomach was suddenly a mass of happy, excited knots.

Charlotte didn't even think about trying to paint that evening. She knew it would be a total waste of time. All she could think about, suddenly, was Jett and what was going to happen once Imelda was gone.

She went for a walk in the garden after a light supper of chicken salad and examined her lingering feelings of guilt. They were needless, she told herself. She had no reason to feel guilty. The affair

had been over before she'd come along and Jett
had assured her anyway that Imelda was not in love
with him. It was just that she was upset about some
problem.

No, Jett was free. Imelda was the past. And, in
a matter of hours, she'd be leaving for good.

Charlotte sat down on one of the garden seats
and stared at the moon, hanging like a silver disc
in the sky. And her heart was suddenly filled with
hope and happiness and dreams she scarcely dared
to dream. What would happen now between her
and Jett?

'Are you making a wish?'

Charlotte jumped as though scalded as a voice
as soft as velvet suddenly spoke at her elbow. She
looked up and felt her heart turn to putty inside
her. The bluest eyes in the world were smiling down
at her.

'Well, were you making a wish?' Jett insisted.

'Not really. Well, sort of.' She felt suddenly
certain that her face must be glowing as brightly as
the moon! She turned away awkwardly. 'I guess I
was just moon-gazing.'

'Do you mind if I join you?' He was seating
himself beside her, his arm brushing against hers,
making her jump out of her skin. 'I'm rather partial
to a bit of moon-gazing myself.'

Charlotte could feel her heart beating like a drum
inside her. She stared hard at the moon, trying to
control it. 'How was your dinner with Imelda?' she
enquired.

'OK,' he shrugged. 'But not half as good as last
night.' Then she felt him smile. 'Nor as good as
tomorrow night,' he added.

Charlotte had intended not to look at him, to keep her gaze fixed on the moon, but in spite of herself her eyes had swivelled to meet his, and instantly she felt swallowed in their endless midnight blueness.

How wonderful he is, she found herself thinking helplessly.

'And what about you? Did you enjoy your dinner?'

As he spoke, he reached out and took her hand in his.

'I had some chicken salad.' Her tongue had turned to cardboard. 'It was very nice,' she added with some difficulty.

'Good.'

He was caressing her hand very softly, his fingers seeming barely to make contact with her own, yet stirring sensations that were fierce and overwhelming and emotions so intense they were almost visible.

Suddenly aware that she was trembling, Charlotte caught her breath, closed her eyes and fought to pull herself together.

'Are you cold?'

As she sat there shivering, he had slipped an arm round her shoulders. He was drawing her against him, offering her his warmth. And she longed to sink against him. More than anything she longed for it. And yet at the same time she feared what might happen if she were to release the storm of pent-up feelings inside her. And so, in spite of herself, she resisted.

'A little,' she croaked, struggling to keep her tone light.

'In that case, I think perhaps we ought to go indoors.' Even as he spoke, he was rising to his feet, his arm still round her, drawing her with him. Then he was shrugging off his jacket and laying it lightly round her shoulders. 'There,' he smiled. 'Is that any better?'

Charlotte nodded, though she feared her trembling had increased. All at once she was overpowered by the wonderful feel of the warm jacket, and the heady scent that rose from it, the scent of his skin.

It was as though suddenly, wonderfully, he was all around her. She felt drunk on the excitement that suddenly poured through her.

'You're still trembling.'

He stood facing her, his arms circling her lightly. She could feel the hardness of his chest brushing against her breasts. Charlotte stared at his tie, afraid to raise her eyes higher. 'I hadn't realised how cold it had got,' she said.

'It gets cool in the evenings at this time of year. You shouldn't have left the house without a sweater.' Jett drew her closer, chafing her shoulders softly. 'Silly girl. What were you thinking of?' he said.

Involuntarily then Charlotte found herself glancing up at him. She had intended to smile lightheartedly, but the smile died on her lips. How could she smile when every inch of her ached with pure longing?

'Sweet Charlotte.'

As he said her name, Jett touched her hair softly, sending wicked little darts of pleasure through her. Then his fingers were moving round to the back of her head, while his other hand drew her even more closely against him.

As dark as velvet in the moonlight, his eyes poured into her, and every muscle in Charlotte's body suddenly seemed to have turned to water. Then everything stood still—even the night stopped breathing—and next moment he was closing his eyes and kissing her.

As his lips pressed against hers, she clung to him tightly, the breath coming in sharp little sobs in her throat. I shall die for the wanting of him, she was thinking. Surely there can be no cure for a need as great as this?

Jett's lips were as hungry as hers, swallowing her, devouring her. And the taste of him was sweeter than the gods' own nectar. Charlotte gasped as their two hungry tongues collided, wickedly, insatiably, exploring one another. Her body shuddering with excitement, she wound her arms round his neck.

His heart was racing in time with hers. She could feel it through his shirt. Releasing one hand, she pressed her palm against his chest, loving the feel of the swift excited beat.

And that was when, making her gasp, he did the same to her. The hand in her hair had come round to cup her breast, causing her whole body to slacken with desire against him. Then with his thumb he was strumming the hard taut peak, lighting a sudden fierce fire in her loins.

Involuntarily, Charlotte pressed her hips against his and gasped at the hard thrust of desire between his legs. More than anything she longed to feel that hardness pierce her flesh.

His hand was still on her breast, and as she felt him undo her blouse buttons, Charlotte held her breath in anticipation. But at the last moment, he paused and refastened the undone buttons and simply held her close for a moment.

'I think we ought to stop there,' he whispered huskily against her ear. 'Or else we'll end up making love right here on this garden seat.' He kissed her cheek softly. 'And I think that would be a mistake. For our first time we ought to pick a more comfortable spot.'

Charlotte could only nod soundlessly. She still felt dizzy with longing. But though he had stopped the helter-skelter, all was not lost.

'For our first time', he had said, his tone full of promise. So he intended there to be a first time—and perhaps many more after that. Soon, possibly very soon, they were going to become lovers.

And somehow that was the only thing that mattered. That sooner or later she would have him. That she would have this wonderful man all to herself.

She smiled happily as he slipped an arm round her waist and proceeded to lead her back to the house. Everything felt right. Everything was falling into place.

They were approaching the patio when he suddenly told her, 'Imelda's decided to leave tomorrow morning.' He caught her eye as he said it and there was no need to say more. They both knew precisely what Imelda's departure would mean.

Then at the foot of the stairs he paused to kiss her. 'Goodnight, Charlotte.' He slipped the jacket from her shoulders and slung it over his arm with a smile. 'You won't be needing this any more.'

'No.' Charlotte smiled back at him. She had no need of any jacket. Her flesh was still tingling where he had touched her, her lips still burning from his kisses. She felt as though she would never need a jacket again. She smiled another small smile. 'Goodnight, Jett,' she said.

And as she climbed the stairs to bed she was glowing like a glow-worm, her body tingling and burning, her very heart alight with happiness. Suddenly she couldn't wait for tomorrow to come.

It was simple politeness that caused Charlotte the following morning to pause on her way past Imelda's room to say goodbye. She might not have another chance after she'd gone to pick up Lucas— not if Imelda was planning to catch the early train.

She tapped lightly on the door. 'Imelda?' she called.

When there was no reply, she opened the door a crack, stuck her head round and glanced curiously round the room. The bed was undone and there was an open suitcase lying on it. Imelda had evidently started packing.

But there was no sign of Imelda. Where had she gone?

It was at that precise moment, as she hesitated in the doorway, that Charlotte became aware of a noise coming from the en-suite bathroom. She stepped quickly into the room with a frown of concern. It sounded as though Imelda was being violently sick.

'Imelda, are you all right?' The bathroom door was slightly open. Charlotte gave a sharp tap. 'May I come in?'

When the only response was another bout of retching, Charlotte didn't hang around. She pushed the door open. 'Imelda, what's going on?' she demanded, stepping inside.

Imelda had been bending over the toilet, her cheeks as pale as tissue paper. She straightened now, slowly, dabbing her mouth with a towel. 'What does it look like?' she said tightly. 'I was being sick.'

'Yes, I can see that. That's why I was worried.' Charlotte frowned at her. 'I really think we ought to call a doctor. Yesterday you fainted and now you're being sick. There's obviously something very wrong with you.'

'There's nothing wrong with me.'

'Imelda, there has to be. Let me speak to Jett. I'll ask him to call a doctor.'

But as she started to turn away, Imelda stopped her in her tracks.

'I don't need a doctor.' She tossed the towel aside, and suddenly the tears were standing in her eyes. 'There's nothing wrong with me. I'm not ill. I'm pregnant.'

CHAPTER EIGHT

'PREGNANT?'

Charlotte blinked at Imelda in astonishment. Such a possibility had never entered her head—though, now that she thought about it, perhaps it ought to have, considering the nature of Imelda's symptoms.

She frowned at the other girl. 'Does Jett know?' she asked.

Imelda had blinked back the tears that had momentarily risen in her eyes. She appeared to be making a huge effort to control herself. Taking a deep breath, she said bitterly, 'Jett was among the first to know.'

Well, that made sense, since he was clearly the father! Charlotte felt a rush of black anger towards him. 'And what did he have to say?' she demanded.

'What do you think he said?' Imelda's lower lip trembled. 'He said I ought to have been more careful.'

'*You* ought to have been more careful? What about him!' Charlotte paused as the tears began to roll down Imelda's cheeks and a sudden sob of misery shook her slender frame. She took the girl in her arms and held her, comforting her. 'What are you going to do?' she asked her kindly.

'I've no idea.' The words came out choked and distorted. 'I came here, hoping...' She broke off with another sob. 'But it's no good. I'm just going to have to deal with it on my own.'

'Oh, Imelda, I'm so sorry.' Charlotte stroked the girl's hair. And though her tone was sympathetic, inside she was seething. How could Jett be so callous? How could he just abandon her? The way he was behaving was a scandal and an outrage.

'I'm going home now to try and get myself together.' Imelda straightened and rubbed the tears from her eyes. Then she glanced at her watch. 'I'd better finish packing. My taxi will be here in quarter of an hour.'

Imelda's taxi arrived just as Charlotte was setting off to pick up Lucas. She waved the girl off, still in a state of deep shock. This changed everything, of course.

It certainly drastically changed her feelings for Jett—who hadn't even shown up to say goodbye to Imelda. Once, she'd thought he was a snake, and now she knew she'd been dead right. There was no other way to describe a man who behaved like that.

So his relationship with Imelda was all over, was it? Something to be forgotten. A thing of the past. And the child she was carrying was a mere 'problem' she was having! Charlotte felt shocked now to remember the things he'd said.

A great sadness suddenly filled her. She'd been so wrong about everything. She'd thought Jett was special. She'd been on the brink of falling in love with him.

Somewhere inside her a door closed painfully. The only decent thing she could feel for him now was disgust.

After she'd dropped Lucas off at the nursery, Charlotte went back to the manor.

The Jaguar, she noticed, was parked outside—which it had not been when she and Imelda had left earlier. So, he was in there, she thought, probably feeling pretty pleased with himself. Well, he was in for a shock. She was about to burst his balloon.

She marched through the front door, bristling with anger. 'Jett!' she called out. 'Jett! Where are you?' Then, when nobody replied, she marched out to the back patio.

But he wasn't there either. She searched the ground floor in vain. Perhaps, she decided, he was upstairs in his room.

She climbed the stairs swiftly, then hesitated at the top. Jett's room was in the west wing, at the other side of the house from where her own was situated and Imelda's had been, and she had never set foot in the west wing before.

Suddenly she felt a little nervous, a bit like a trespasser. Was it wise, she wondered, to approach him in the privacy of his own room?

That's silly, she told herself. Why should I be nervous? After all, it's not as though I'm planning to seduce him! In fact, quite the opposite! I'm planning to tear him limb from limb!

On that reassuring thought, she headed boldly along the west wing corridor, that was flooded with light from the casement window at the far end. His room was probably the last one, overlooking the rear gardens, she decided, as she headed for the door at the end.

'You're looking lovely this morning.'

His voice came from behind her. Charlotte swung round to face him. 'Where did you come from?'

But even as she asked, she'd figured out the answer. He had evidently just emerged from the room behind him. The door stood ajar, though she hadn't heard it open.

'I was in there,' he nodded, confirming her theory. 'I heard footsteps that didn't sound like Annie's.' He paused. 'Well, I must say this is a nice surprise.'

His form was silhouetted sharply in the light from the casement window—the broad shoulders, the long legs, the head of thick dark hair. And he looked so striking it almost took Charlotte's breath away. How can anyone who looks so fabulous be so rotten? she wondered sadly.

That thought reminded her of her mission. She said, 'I suppose you know Imelda's gone?'

'Is that why you're here?' He smiled a wicked smile at her and slipped his hands into his trouser pockets. 'I must say I find your eagerness extremely flattering.'

Charlotte blushed to her hair roots and felt her stomach turn over. 'No, that's not why I'm here, so don't bother being flattered.'

She tore her eyes away from him and sought to still her churning stomach. Though it was sheer revulsion, surely, that had caused it to churn? Knowing what she now knew about Jett Ashton, how could she possibly find him attractive?

He was still standing there watching her with a smile of amusement. 'Then, why are you here?' he wanted to know.

'I wanted to ask you——' She had to take a deep breath. Did he have no shame that he could stand there and smile like that? 'I wanted to ask you where you were when Imelda left this morning. I thought you might have had the decency at least to say goodbye.'

The blue eyes widened a little. He had not expected this rebuke. But his gaze never flickered. He said, 'I was elsewhere.'

'So it would seem. Don't you think that was a little lax of you? Don't you think you ought to have been there at least to wave her off?'

'Lax?' Jett seemed to find her choice of word amusing. He tilted his head at her, his smile curling at the corners. 'No, as a matter of fact I don't think it was lax. I had to be somewhere else and I'd already said my goodbyes last night. I consider one set of goodbyes to be quite sufficient.'

At that moment the phone in the room behind him began to ring. 'Excuse me one minute.' He headed back into the room to answer it, leaving Charlotte standing in the corridor.

Who was it? she wondered. Was it Imelda? She fancied she could hear the poor girl sobbing down the phone.

In actual fact she heard nothing, just a few meaningless words from Jett. She wasn't even aware that he'd hung up until he stuck his head round the door and beckoned to her.

'I suppose you'd better come in,' he said.

The room was an elegant study, small and charming, with a tan leather sofa against one wall, a Queen Anne bureau in one corner and a collection of framed prints arranged on the walls.

Jett was standing by the bureau, his back half turned to her, as he scribbled something on a piece of paper. 'You may be interested to know what I was doing,' he said now, 'when I was so rudely interrupted by the sound of your footsteps along the corridor.'

Charlotte did not respond. She was not remotely interested, as he would have seen from her expression had he bothered to turn round.

But he told her anyway. 'I was making out a list of all the items that have disappeared over the past couple of years. Paintings, bronzes, porcelain, silver...' He flicked her a look then as he tossed aside his fountain pen. 'You may remember I mentioned before about the things that have gone missing? Well, you'd be surprised how long the list turns out to be.'

Charlotte felt shocked and angry as she looked back at him in silence. Less than an hour ago his pregnant, discarded girlfriend had left his house in a flood of tears and all he could think about were some paintings that had disappeared!

'Is that so?' Charlotte threw him a cold look. Then she drew herself up tall and looked him in the eye. 'I know about Imelda,' she told him candidly. 'Before she left, she told me she was pregnant.'

Jett straightened then and turned round fully to face her. 'Oh, really?' he responded. 'And what was your reaction?'

'Shock, initially. Surprise and sadness.'

'Surprise and sadness?' Jett smiled a bitter smile. 'Mine, I'm afraid, was something rather closer to anger.'

Charlotte felt her lips tighten. 'Anger?' she said scathingly. 'I see you consider contraception to be the responsibility of the woman? Isn't that a rather convenient point of view?'

'It may be.' The sapphire-blue eyes had narrowed. Charlotte could sense he disliked her tone of disapproval. 'But since it's the woman who runs the risk of getting pregnant, I would say it's a responsibility it's in her interests to accept.'

There was a lot of truth in that. Charlotte couldn't argue with it. But she still wasn't about to let him off the hook.

She threw him a hard look. 'But accidents can happen, even when the woman has taken responsibility. Are you saying that, even then, the man should get off scot-free?'

'No, I'm not saying that. Of course he shouldn't. But that isn't the situation we're talking about here.'

As he straightened, Charlotte could sense the angry emotion in him that he was suddenly having to struggle to keep under control. He had seemed totally detached, but she could see now that he was not. There was a seething, white-hot fury inside him that sprang from his eyes and bubbled from every pore.

He said, 'What we're talking about is not some accident. What we're talking about is something very different—a young woman who deliberately got herself pregnant in order to try and bag herself a rich husband.'

The blue eyes flashed. 'I think you'll agree that puts things in a rather different light.'

It did, if it was true. If it was true, it was shocking. If it was true, then Imelda was totally to blame.

Charlotte felt stunned by his accusation, but at the same time sceptical. 'Why should I believe you?' she asked him, frowning.

'Believe what you like.' Suddenly Jett seemed to lose patience. He turned away and scooped up some papers from the bureau, folded them in two and stuffed them into a manila envelope. 'Believe what you like,' he told her again, 'but let's drop the subject, if you don't mind. Frankly,' he added, making an illustrative gesture with his hand, 'I've had Imelda and her wretched pregnancy up to here.'

'Yes, I can see that.'

Charlotte's tone was still censorious. She wanted to believe that what he'd told her was true. If it was true, it made him much less of a monster. But she still found his attitude shockingly callous. He spoke as though he had nothing to do with this unborn child. As though it was an alien being and not his own flesh and blood.

As he reached for his jacket that hung on the back of the bureau chair, pulled it on and stuffed the envelope into one of the pockets, Charlotte watched him, suddenly seeing him as though through the wrong end of a telescope.

He seemed suddenly very distant. Physically close, yet miles away. He might as well have been on the far side of the moon.

In a small voice she asked him, 'So what will happen to the child?'

'I have no idea.' He regarded her stonily. 'The best I can do is see that it's supported financially.'

He pulled a tight, uncompassionate smile. 'And wish that it might have been born to a better mother.'

And to a better father. Charlotte thought it, though she did not say it. Just the thought was already quite cruel enough. It had felt like a rapier-thrust to her heart.

'And now, if you don't mind, I have business in town.' Jett was glancing at his watch and motioning her towards the door. 'Business, I'm extremely happy to say, that has nothing whatsoever to do with Imelda.'

Without another word, Charlotte passed obediently through the doorway, then headed silently down the corridor towards the landing. And as Jett swept past her, she paused for a moment to look at him.

It really was true what Ted and Ellen had always told her. He cared about nothing. And she found that shocking.

But what shocked her even more were her own emotions. For though it shamed her to the core, she couldn't help it. She still wanted him, desperately, in spite of everything.

The rest of the morning, for Charlotte, passed in a kind of daze as she paced up and down, endlessly, in her room. She felt confused and edgy, unable to concentrate on anything.

She kept thinking of Imelda and her unborn baby, and of Jett's callous attitude to the whole situation. How could she want a man like that?

It was a relief when it was time to go and collect Lucas. The child's chirpy company, she hoped, would distract her—and without some kind of distraction her brain would soon explode! It was just going round in circles, getting nowhere.

And the child's company did prove a welcome tonic. As they drove from the nursery back to the Coach House and Lucas told her all about the finger puppets he'd been making, for the first time that day Charlotte felt herself relax.

But not for long. A surprise awaited her at the Coach House.

'What on earth are you doing here? Why aren't you at work?' Charlotte blinked as Ellen appeared to greet them in the hallway. Then she frowned with concern into the woman's pale face. 'Are you all right, Ellen? What's the matter? Are you ill?'

Ellen didn't bother to answer. She clutched at Charlotte's arm. 'It's Jett,' she stammered. 'He's summoned Ted up to the manor. It's serious, Charlotte. I'm so afraid.'

Charlotte patted Ellen's hand. 'Calm down,' she told her. Then she turned to Lucas, who was frowning up at his mother. 'You go out into the back garden and play,' she told him. 'I want to have a private word with your mother.'

'OK.' Unconcerned, Lucas skipped off obediently, and instantly Charlotte turned her attention back to Ellen.

'What's going on?' she demanded. 'What's this about Jett and Ted?'

Five minutes later she was climbing back into her car and racing the short distance up to the manor. And she only just missed by a fraction of a centimetre colliding head-on with Ted's rusty old

Vauxhall as it came hurtling past in the opposite direction.

Things looked bad, she thought anxiously, drawing up alongside Jett's sleek Jaguar. Ellen hadn't been exaggerating, after all.

She had her second near-collision in the hallway—this time with Jett as he came storming down the stairs.

He flung her an impatient look. 'What the devil are you doing here?' Then he flew past her like a tornado. 'Get out of my way!'

He was heading for the drawing-room. Charlotte hurried after him. 'What's going on?' she demanded. 'Ellen tells me you've evicted them, that they've got to be out of the house by the end of the week.'

'Then you've no need to come here asking me what's going on! It seems as if Ellen has already told you!'

'What I want to know is why!' He hadn't slowed his pace and Charlotte was almost having to run to keep up with him. 'Why this sudden rush to throw them out of their home? Surely, at least, you could give them a little more time?'

Jett had come to a halt beside the bar table. He picked up one of the decanters and poured a stiff Scotch. 'I'm not in the habit of drinking whisky at lunchtime.' As he took a quick swig, he tossed a wry smile at Charlotte. 'But after today's little showdown I feel like making an exception.'

Charlotte pulled a face. She suspected he was not alone. Back at the Coach House, Ted was probably having a stiff drink himself! From the way he'd been driving, he'd been pretty upset.

She frowned now at Jett as he crossed to one of the sofas and sank down against the cushions with an audible sigh. 'Can't you rethink your decision? Aren't you being a little hasty? As I said, at least give them a bit more time.'

Jett released another sigh, this time of sheer impatience, and Charlotte could sense the long tanned fingers curling more tightly round his glass.

In a sharp tone he told her, 'Why don't you go and do some painting?' His eyes flicked up to meet hers. 'And mind your own damned business for a change?'

Charlotte glared at him. 'Well, at least no one could accuse you of subtlety! But you're not going to get rid of me as easily as that.' She took a couple of steps towards him. 'I consider it is my business. Ellen and Ted are my friends and I love their little boy. I can't just stand by and let you throw them out of their house.'

'So you keep saying.' Jett took another swig of whisky. 'So, tell me, what do you plan to do about it?'

Now it was Charlotte's turn to sigh as she met the steely blue gaze. What could she do? She felt suddenly quite powerless. She could rant and rave at him till she was blue in the face, but it wouldn't make a jot of difference, she suspected. He was totally immune to her ranting and raving.

She took a deep breath and tried to calm her racing heart, lowering her tone to a gentle entreaty.

'Look, I know you're wrong in what you think about Ted. But I'm not asking you to take my word for it,' she hurried on, as with a flash of impatience Jett threatened to interrupt her. 'All I'm asking is that you just take a bit more time, do some more checking up... and you'll see that I'm right.'

'And in the meantime...' Her eyes were quite openly begging him. 'In the meantime, let them stay on at the Coach House. Don't throw them out. That would be a terrible thing to do.'

There was a moment of silence as Charlotte held her breath and Jett, very deliberately, drained his whisky glass.

'Nice speech. I'm deeply moved.' He leaned forward in his seat and laid his glass on the coffee table in front of him. Then his gaze flicked up, flinty-hard, to meet hers again. 'However, I'm afraid the answer is no can do.'

'How can you say that? How can you do that?'

'Very easily.'

'But it's shocking! It's monstrous!'

'You may think so. I think differently. And nothing you can say is going to change that.'

'But you can't! You can't!' She felt like falling on her knees to him. 'Think of Lucas! Think of what this will do to him! Surely, you wouldn't throw a poor, innocent child out of his home!'

There was no reaction in his eyes. He simply looked back at her, his expression as cold as a polar icecap. 'I've made my decision and my decision is final. I warn you all you're doing is wasting your breath.'

And he really meant it. Every crushing, heartless word of it. As she looked into his face, Charlotte felt her blood go cold.

What a fool she'd been. She'd thought he'd grown to care for Lucas, that his relationship with the little boy would count for something. But she'd been crazy. She'd only believed what she'd wanted to believe. It was unlikely, after all, that he could really care for Lucas when he was incapable of feeling anything for his own unborn child.

She felt a passion of anger rise up inside her as she looked into his handsome, cold-hearted face and suddenly she could hold back her emotions no longer.

'You're evil!' she spat at him. 'You're evil and unnatural! Blood ties mean nothing to you! All you care about is possessions!'

She snatched an angry breath. 'Well, I'll tell you something ... I'm not staying under your roof for one minute longer! The very idea turns my stomach.' She swung round on her heel. 'I'm going upstairs to pack!'

But she had only got two steps when she stopped in her tracks. Suddenly, through the sitting-room doorway, rushed a distraught, weeping Ellen.

'Ted's taken Lucas!' The tears were pouring down her face. 'He drove off with him just a couple of minutes ago.' She glared dementedly at Jett. 'And it's all your fault! He says he won't return him until you change your mind. You made him do it! You're the one to blame!'

Jett had sprung to his feet. 'Did he say where he was taking him?' In two steps he was standing before the sobbing, pale-faced woman. 'Did he give you any clue at all?'

Tearfully, Ellen shook her head. 'I've no idea where they've gone.'

There was a moment of helpless silence. Charlotte almost felt like weeping. Poor Lucas. What a terrible thing to have happened.

But then a thunderbolt struck her. Wide-eyed, she looked at Jett. 'I'll bet I know where Ted's taken Lucas!' she declared.

She snatched a breath and glanced at Ellen. 'His friend's cabin down in Cornwall... That place where he goes on fishing weekends...' Her eyes glowed with conviction. 'I'll bet that's where he's gone!'

Jett was frowning at Ellen. 'Do you know where it is?'

But Ellen shook her head despondently. 'No, not really.'

Then Charlotte cut in again. 'I think I do,' she said excitedly. 'I once asked Ted about it and he gave me a pretty good description.'

The words were barely out before Jett had grabbed hold of her. 'You've just got yourself a job as my navigator!' he told her. 'You and I are going to find them!'

Then he was propelling her across the room, through the hall and out to the driveway, where the big sleek Jaguar was parked. A moment later he was grabbing open the passenger door and shoving her unceremoniously inside. Then he was climbing in beside her, switching on the engine and, with an ear-splitting squeal of tyres, they were off.

He turned for an instant to shoot her a look. 'Let's see if I can count on your co-operation for once!'

CHAPTER NINE

'IN LUCAS'S interests, naturally, I'll co-operate.'
Charlotte regarded Jett tightly as they sped towards the main road. 'Though I know that saving
Lucas is not what concerns you. All you're
interested in is catching Ted.'

'What a smart girl you are.' Jett darted a quick
glance at her. 'You've really got me pretty shrewdly
summed up.'

'Yes, I have.'

More's the pity, she added to herself. For, now
that she understood him and how rotten he was,
living with her feelings for him was growing more
and more difficult.

Even now, she thought despairingly, staring out
of the window, not daring to look at him in case
that made the feeling worse, she was aware of a
treacherous warm glow round her heart just to be
sitting here in the car beside him. He was like some
viral infection that she just couldn't shake off.

'But let's just leave aside our personal warm
feelings for the moment——' Jett's tone was full of
heavy sarcasm '—and concentrate instead on the
job in hand.'

He paused and flicked a look at her. 'Tell me
everything you remember about where this cabin is
that Ted goes to in Cornwall. Every single detail
you recall.'

Charlotte told him, dredging her memory to the limit, and even she was impressed by how much detail she managed to come up with. It was amazing what one was capable of in an emergency!

'Good girl.' Jett nodded his approval at her. 'On that description I'd say we'll find the cabin no bother.' Then, unexpectedly, he reached out and very quickly squeezed her arm. 'Don't worry,' he told her. 'We're going to find them. You can set your mind at rest on that.'

At the touch of him, Charlotte felt her heart turn over. And there was something in his eyes, a flicker of warm sympathy, that just for a moment made her catch her breath.

He actually looked as though he cared as much as she did. As though it was not just anger and spite that had sent him on this mission, but some far kinder, more compassionate emotion. It was as though he really did care for Lucas's welfare and was sharing the anxiety that filled poor Charlotte's heart. For a moment she felt bound to him by the emotions they seemed to share.

But almost instantly Charlotte pushed the feeling from her. That sensation of oneness was false and misleading, a mere product of her currently over-wrought emotional state.

Yet she was shocked at how deeply the sensation had touched her. Pushing it away had felt like an immense and painful loss. More than anything she had wanted to go on feeling that close to him. To hang on to that bond that had seemed briefly to bind them.

It had felt rather like that time he'd lent her his jacket. Warm and intimate and natural and complete. Now that the feeling had gone, her heart felt cold.

Stop it! Charlotte clenched her fists in her lap and kept her eyes fixed straight ahead through the windscreen. Don't think such thoughts. They're mad! she chastised herself.

Just think of Lucas and what we're here to do. And pray that we get to Cornwall soon.

As it turned out they didn't have to go as far as Cornwall. They were passing a roadside café, less than thirty miles along the road, when Jett spotted Ted's old Vauxhall in the car park.

'They're in there!' With a quick manoeuvre he had turned off the main road and was slotting the big Jaguar into a space in the car park. He turned to Charlotte. 'We're going inside. You look after Lucas and just leave me to deal with Ted.'

Charlotte nodded. 'OK.' That sounded like a reasonable plan of action. 'Just make sure——' she began. But she got no further. Jett was already jumping out of the car.

'Hey, wait for me!' Charlotte jumped out after him and hurried across the car park behind him as he headed on swift strides for the café. 'Just make sure——' she began again, intending to exhort him not to provoke any violent or distressing scenes. Lucas had had more than enough upset for one day. But she never finished the sentence, for suddenly all hell broke loose.

'There he is, damn him!'

Jett pointed to the café doorway, where Ted had appeared with Lucas at his side. But as Jett started to stride towards them, Ted suddenly spotted him. Charlotte saw him blanche and freeze to the spot.

But he didn't remain frozen for long. The very next instant he was darting out of the doorway, zig-zagging to avoid Jett's clutches, making a desperate bid to get back to his car.

And that was when the unexpected happened.

Jett could easily have caught Ted if he'd gone after him. He was fitter and faster. Ted wouldn't have stood a chance.

And he'd been on the point of going after him when suddenly little Lucas, left alone and abandoned in the café doorway, had burst into a helpless flood of tears. 'Daddy!' he wailed, his face crumpling in dismay.

There was no hesitation. Jett seemed to act without thinking. 'Don't worry, I'm here.' Suddenly he was calling to the little boy, stepping towards him and sweeping him up into his arms. 'Don't cry. It's all right. Daddy's had to go away. But Uncle Jett is here to look after you now.'

A lump had flown to Charlotte's throat as she watched the little scene. She could scarcely believe what she was seeing. Jett's first thought, astonishingly, had been for the child. Out of compassion for Lucas he'd let his victim go.

As she hurried up to join him, she looked into his face, bewildered and warmed by what she'd just seen. 'I'll look after Lucas now, if you want to go after Ted,' she offered, reaching out her arms to take the child.

But Jett shook his head. 'Let him go for the moment. There's no hurry, I can go after him later.'

He smiled and affectionately ruffled the child's hair. 'The important thing is we've got Lucas back.'

The journey back to the Coach House was light-hearted and jolly, with Jett doing an admirable job of keeping Lucas amused. Before they were even halfway there the child appeared to have forgotten all about his brief adventure.

And Charlotte was feeling a great deal better, too.

'You look transformed,' Jett told her, turning to smile across at her. 'I've never seen anyone look more anxious than you did when we first set off on our little search. What's the matter?' he winked at her. 'Didn't you think I'd find them?'

'I *knew* you'd find them.' And it was absolutely true. That was something she'd never doubted for a moment. Jett was the type of man who got what he went after!

'I guess I was shocked,' she confessed. 'I couldn't believe Ted could do that. I mean, to have so little regard for his own child . . .'

She let the sentence trail off, as it suddenly occurred to her that she was speaking to a man who had even less regard for his. His own unborn child to him was just a 'problem'. She felt a shiver go through her as she remembered.

And his attitude towards Lucas was just as hard-hearted. Wasn't he threatening to throw the child out on the street?

The warm, relieved feeling inside her began to crumble. She sat back a little more stiffly in her seat. Back there at the café he had shown a spark of humanity in the way he had instantly gone to Lucas. But that had been a brief and fleeting moment. Whatever humanity he possessed was no more than skin deep.

His eyes were on her. 'You're frowning again,' he told her. 'And you know I don't like it when you frown. Come on. I want to see a smile.'

The words tugged at her heart. That tone of easy familiarity was the hardest thing in the world to bear. It made her melt and shrivel with despair simultaneously. So near, she thought miserably, and yet so far.

Still, she managed to conjure up a fair imitation of a smile. 'Happy now?' she demanded, mock teasing.

His eyes held hers a moment and there was a strange expression there, almost as though he could read the thoughts in her head. Then he turned back to the road with a nod of his head,

'It'll do,' he told her. 'For the moment.'

Back at the Coach House Ellen was waiting, and as soon as she saw Lucas she burst into tears.

'Oh, thank God!' she breathed, hugging her child to her bosom. Then she glanced up through her tears at Jett and Charlotte. 'Thank you—both of you,' she said.

Charlotte smiled back at her reassuringly. 'He seems to be none the worse for his adventure.'

She started to turn away, about to say, 'We'll leave you now', but before she could Jett was catching her by the arm.

'I won't come with you. I'd like an hour alone with Ellen.' He held her for a moment, his eyes pouring down on her with a look of urgent, almost anxious, entreaty. 'But don't go anywhere. You and I need to talk.'

What on earth about? And why that look in his eyes? What could he suddenly have to say to her that was so important?

But as his fingers burned into her like firebrands, she nodded. 'OK,' she promised him. 'I'll be waiting.' Whatever it was, she intended to find out!

The hour of waiting for him seemed endless.

Charlotte sat out on the patio and tried to relax, but her brain was going round in circles. What was going on? What was happening down at the Coach House? And what would Jett have to say to her when he finally arrived? One question followed another, and the questions were endless.

For the five millionth time, she glanced at her watch. Come on, Jett! she urged silently. Come and put me out of my agony!

'I'm sorry you had to wait so long.'

As he suddenly spoke, Charlotte jumped. She swivelled round to find him watching her from the drawing-room doorway.

Charlotte blinked at him foolishly. 'I wasn't doing anything else.'

'I'm afraid I had to talk to Ellen first.' He had stepped out on to the patio and was seating himself in one of the white-painted chairs opposite her. 'It seemed Ted had relayed a somewhat inaccurate account of the conversation we had this morning.'

Charlotte could feel her heart lurching about inside her. That urgent look of before still burned in his eyes. In fact, there was a sense of urgency about his whole demeanour. What he was about to tell her was clearly something important—and something that he urgently wanted her to hear.

She felt a sudden, illogical twist of hope inside her. Would she no longer feel obliged to hate him after she'd heard it?

Jett was stretching his long legs out in front of him. He frowned at her. 'I suppose you've been wondering what's going on?'

'Yes, you could say that.' Charlotte smiled back at him wryly. 'And I'm rather hoping you plan to tell me.'

'I'm afraid it's rather a long story.'

'I don't mind. I want to hear it.'

'Good. I think it's time we cleared a couple of things up.'

As his eyes held hers, the hope in Charlotte flared more brightly. What he's going to tell me will change everything, she was thinking.

She leaned forward in her seat. 'Go on,' she urged him. Suddenly, her heart was beating very fast.

Jett took a deep breath. 'OK. Here we go. But I'm afraid you're not going to like this first bit. You see, I was right about Ted and you were wrong.'

'You mean he has been stealing?'

Charlotte frowned at him. Jett was right, she didn't like the accusation. But she no longer felt inclined to reject it out of hand. Ted's flight with Lucas had rather poisoned her view of him. She had not believed him to be the type of man who would callously hold his small son to ransom and subject him to all the traumas that could spring from such an action. And if she'd been wrong about that, she could be wrong about other things. She held her breath and waited as Jett carried on.

'Yes, I'm afraid he has been stealing. Let me explain...' Jett paused for a moment and ran his fingers through his hair, and a dark shadow seemed to fall across his eyes. As Charlotte watched him she felt a stab of compassion. Clearly, he was finding this whole thing deeply painful.

'What happened was this...' Jett drew himself up in his chair. 'The paintings and things were sold to pay for repairs... That bit, to some extent, is accurate enough. But what is wildly inaccurate are the sums written in the manor's account books that supposedly record the prices that were paid.'

He broke off to shake his head. 'The pieces were sold privately, rather than at auction, in order to save embarrassment, so Ted claimed at the time. But the real reason for selling privately was so that he could keep secret the sums of money that actually changed hands. He would sell a painting for twenty thousand, enter it in the books as fifteen thousand and keep the remaining five thousand for himself.

'He'd been doing it for years, ever since he moved to the Coach House.' A smile as bitter as aloes touched Jett's lips. 'And, of course, it was in order to carry out this little scam that he persuaded Uncle Oscar to let him move there in the first place. I can assure you the arrangement wasn't my uncle's idea.'

Charlotte felt shocked to her marrow. 'What's he been doing with the money? He certainly hasn't been spending any of it!'

'No, he hasn't. He's been investing it.' Jett smiled tightly. 'In more artwork from Penforth Manor, to be precise. Stuff that he's sitting on until the time's right to sell.'

As Charlotte frowned, he proceeded to explain what he meant by that.

'Ted knew he had only a limited amount of time. Once Uncle Oscar was dead the game would be over.' Jett smiled a grim smile and carefully pointed out what no one in their right mind could possibly disagree with. 'He knew he wouldn't be able to get away with it once the estate passed to me. So he had to amass as much as he could while he still had time.'

'So, what did he do? What do you mean he "invested"?' Charlotte was sitting on the edge of her seat.

'What he did was this... He chose a selection of artworks, but instead of putting them on the market all in a rush and possibly not getting as high a price as he might, he hid them away with the intention of hanging on to them until the right buyer came along.

'Of course, he pretended to have sold them, naturally for much less than the price he eventually hoped to get for them...'

'And in the meantime...' Suddenly Charlotte was putting two and two together. 'In the meantime, he used the money he'd fiddled from the other paintings to balance the books of the estate.'

'Clever girl.' Jett smiled across at her. 'That's precisely what he did.'

'So, that means he has a secret cache of artworks hidden away somewhere!' Charlotte paused as a thought struck her. 'Does Ellen know about all this?'

'She does now, alas.' Jett shook his head in sorrow. 'To begin with, I must confess, I assumed

she must be in on it, but I gradually began to realise I was wrong about that. I hated to tell her—
the poor woman was shocked—but in the end I had
no choice.'

'No, I don't suppose you did.' Poor Ellen,
Charlotte was thinking, suddenly to find herself
married to such a criminal.

She glanced across at Jett, grey eyes narrowed.
'I suppose that's why you wanted to evict them?
And I can see that Ted deserved to be thrown out.
But surely Ellen and Lucas didn't?' she added
accusingly.

'No, they didn't, and I never intended to evict
them.' Jett leaned forward suddenly in his chair to
look at her. 'And this is the bit I really wanted you
to hear. You see, I'm really not the monster you
seem to think I am.'

It really mattered to him that she believed that,
Charlotte thought, delighted. And it mattered to
her equally that it was true. As their eyes held a
moment something fierce passed between them—a
mutual, urgent soul-deep desire to smash down the
barriers that stood between them. A desire to reach
out. To touch one another.

Charlotte held her breath. 'Go on,' she said.

Jett continued to hold her gaze. 'I warned Ted
last autumn that I had serious suspicions that he
was up to something. It seemed to me that there
were just too many repairs being done. But, of
course, he denied everything, and it wasn't until a
few months ago that I actually managed to work
out what was going on.'

With a sigh he continued, 'I approached Ted and
told him that if he returned the things he'd stolen

I wouldn't go to the police. Of course, he didn't return them. He said I couldn't prove anything. So that was when I started to get tough with him ...

'I told him that if he refused to return the stuff I'd have no choice but to evict him and his family from the Coach House.' Jett pulled a face. 'I would never have done it, but what I was hoping was that with that threat hanging over him Ted would capitulate in order to save Ellen and Lucas. Needless to say, he didn't—not even when I turned the final screw and told him they'd have to go by the end of the month.'

He shrugged sadly. 'And that's it. You know the story from there.'

And it was quite a story, and a shocking one at that. A story of greed and betrayal and deception. But there was one glimmer of brightness that was warming Charlotte's heart. Jett had never intended to evict Lucas and Ellen. He cared, after all. She could see it in his eyes.

Feeling a weight slip from her shoulders, she looked across at him. 'So, what happens now?' she wanted to know.

'Ah, now, I'm afraid, the police are involved. I called them on the car phone after I'd spoken to Ellen and told them the whole story from start to finish. No doubt they're on their way now to that cabin in Cornwall—for that's where the stuff's being kept, I'm absolutely sure of it.'

He smiled. 'You're the last person I expected to assist me—but it's you I have to thank for dropping that last piece of the puzzle into place.'

Then his expression changed. He leaned forward in his chair. 'I hope you believe all of what I've just told you?'

'Oh, yes. Every word.' Charlotte felt her heart turn over at the look of relief that settled in his eyes. She heard herself say, 'I don't think you're a monster now. In fact, I'm beginning to think you're rather a nice man.'

Then, as he smiled, she blushed to the roots of her hair. The way she'd said it had sounded perhaps a little too admiring!

But who cared? she thought, suddenly smiling back at him. He clearly didn't. In fact he looked quite delighted. All at once, a wonderful sense of joy was pouring through her. He was not a monster and she didn't have to hate him.

Then, as she looked at him, she felt a quick pang of guilt. 'I've been so unfair to you,' she told him. 'All those dreadful stories that Ted and Ellen told me ... I should never have listened. I should have judged you for myself.'

'Not to worry. We've plenty of time to put things right.' Still smiling, Jett leaned forward and clasped her hands in his. 'And we can start tonight. Remember, we have a dinner date ... ? Tonight can be the first step in getting to know each other properly.'

Charlotte had forgotten about their dinner date, but now she glowed at the prospect. 'That sounds like a very good idea to me.'

Jett squeezed her hands and gazed at her a moment. 'But now, I'm afraid I have to leave you. I have an appointment at the local police station. I said I'd go to them rather than them coming to me.' He glanced at his watch. 'I don't know how long I'll be, but how about if we arrange to leave here about eight? I'll book a table for eight-thirty.'

'Sounds fine.'

He winked at her. 'I'll take you somewhere really special.'

As he began to rise to his feet, automatically, Charlotte stood up, too. She felt in perfect tune with him, both mentally and physically, as though everything about them had suddenly been synchronised. As though they were connected to one another by some invisible force.

And it was an utterly, gloriously wonderful feeling, she decided as she stood at the door and waved him off, her lips still tingling where he had kissed her. It felt rather like being halfway to heaven.

After Jett had gone, Charlotte went down to the Coach House to see how Ellen was bearing up in the crisis. She found her shaken but resolute, bravely determined to pull through.

Over a cup of tea she told Charlotte, 'My mother's coming to stay with me. Just for a few weeks, to look after Lucas and give me a bit of moral support.'

Then she added, her expression pained and apologetic, 'Of course, I won't be able to keep you on now. I suppose you realise that? I'm terribly sorry.'

Up until that moment Charlotte hadn't even considered that question, but of course she could see that Ellen had no choice.

'That's OK,' she told her. 'It was only temporary, anyway. And I have a job up in London I'm due to start soon.'

'Does that mean you'll be leaving immediately? I'll be sorry to see you go.'

'Not immediately, no. I have an arrangement with Jett, so I'll be staying on at the manor for another week or so.'

'Oh, good.' Ellen smiled. 'I hope you'll keep in touch. Drop in any time. I know Lucas would love to see you.'

Charlotte pondered on these thoughts as she walked back to the manor. It was rather strange to realise that, soon, she'd be leaving here. She'd become so involved she felt she belonged.

But that was an illusion. She did not belong at all. And, once she left, she would probably never return.

She quickened her footsteps and tried to push away the cold, draughty feeling that thought awakened in her heart. And suddenly, fearfully, she was beginning to wonder if this dinner with Jett tonight was a good idea, after all.

Today she had felt a fragile bond between them. And, tonight, she sensed, it would draw them closer. But, long before it had time to grow strong, that fragile bond was destined to be broken. Soon, too soon, it would be time to say goodbye.

Jett certainly kept his promise to take her somewhere special. Just before eight-thirty they swept through the gates of the Michelin-starred Ludgrove Country House Hotel.

Charlotte let out a gasp of surprise and pleasure. 'I've heard about this place and I've always wanted to come, but I'm afraid it's rather beyond my pocket.' Her eyes widened as they approached the floodlit mansion with its ivy-covered walls and handsome ancient turrets. 'Oh, how wonderful! It's even more beautiful than I expected!'

The food, too, lived up to its reputation. Charlotte had chosen a mouth-watering savoury soufflé to start and was now halfway through the most delicious poached salmon she'd ever tasted.

'This is superb,' she told Jett, her eyes shining happily as she washed it down with a mouthful of equally superb wine. 'I think it's the best meal I've ever tasted.'

Jett smiled across at her and teased, 'Almost as good as the one you cooked for me the other evening.'

Had it only been the other evening? It seemed like an age ago! Charlotte shook her head and smiled back in response. 'I think you're flattering me ... though I confess I didn't do badly.'

'You did excellently. I was most impressed.'

Charlotte had to fight hard to stop herself blushing, and reflected that she'd been fighting back blushes all evening. She couldn't help it. His company delighted her. It seemed everything he said made the blood rush to her head.

It was partly, she decided, because he was looking so gorgeous—in a slim dark suit, cream shirt and blue tie, that matched almost exactly the wonderful colour of his eyes. Every female head in the room had turned admiringly as the two of them were shown to their table. She had never felt so proud to be seen at any man's side.

And she could see in his eyes that she wasn't looking bad either. She'd worn her dressiest outfit— black trousers and a floaty top in dark blues and purples that looked rather striking with her blonde hair.

But what made her beautiful was the glow of excited happiness that shone from her eyes and lit up her face. And the one who was responsible for that was Jett.

They'd had a wonderful evening, light-hearted and full of warmth, like two people who'd never exchanged a cross word in their lives. And there was that feeling, too, of being in perfect tune with one another as they chatted about everything under the sun, exchanging glances and laughing with one another.

But as Jett leaned forward now to pour them both more wine, suddenly there was the hint of a frown in his eyes.

'You know, you really must have thought I was a monster,' he put to her, 'if you believed I'd have thrown Ellen and Lucas out of their home. Did you really think I'd do that to an innocent child?'

Charlotte had to confess she had, though it seemed ludicrous now. She pulled a face and told him, 'You made me believe it. Every time I accused you, you didn't deny it.'

'You're right, I didn't—but there was a reason for that.' Jett reached across the table and took hold of her hand. 'I knew you were friendly with them and I didn't want it getting back to Ted that I had no intention of carrying out my threats. Remember, I was trying to persuade him to co-operate?'

'Yes, I understand that now.' Charlotte felt a shiver go through her as his long brown fingers twined with hers. 'But you really made a good job of making me think you were pretty heartless.'

Jett shook his head. 'Sometimes I wish I was heartless. This whole business would have been much easier if I were.' He sighed. 'If only you knew the sleepless nights I've had worrying about the morality of separating Lucas from his father—which is what will happen if Ted goes to gaol. For me that was the hardest thing to come to terms with.'

Charlotte regarded him with sympathy. 'I can understand that. But the blame is Ted's, not yours,' she assured him in a firm tone. 'He was the one who created the situation that put his relationship with his son in jeopardy.'

'That's what I figured, too.' Jett glanced away for a moment. Suddenly, there was a distant, pre-occupied look in his eyes. 'But a child needs a father. That's what I believe, anyway. I think it's a tragedy when the two can't be together.'

As Charlotte listened, she experienced a sudden flash of mixed emotions. He's thinking of his own unborn son, she decided. Imelda's child. The child he's rejected.

She cleared her throat. 'I think so, too. But if a father really wants to, he can keep in touch with his child. The bond between them needn't be broken.'

As he looked up at her, frowning a little, she added quickly, 'There's no reason why Ted need lose touch with Lucas.' Jett might resent it if he suspected she was getting personal. For this was one subject that, up till now, they hadn't touched on.

'It's his duty to keep in touch.' Jett glanced down at their twined fingers. 'As the child's father, it's no less than his bounden duty.'

'You believe that?'

'Of course I do.'

'You believe it of any father? I mean even in cases where the parents aren't married?'

She held her breath as he looked up at her then. She hadn't meant to say that. That had very definitely been personal.

But instead of responding with annoyance as she'd half expected, Jett surprised her by smiling back at her fleetingly.

'Oh, yes,' he assured her. 'Whatever the circumstances, I believe a father has a duty to participate in the raising of his offspring.'

Charlotte was aware of a sense of relief rushing through her. So he did not intend to abandon his child, after all. This appeared to be another point on which she had misjudged him. Thank heavens, she thought. I wasn't happy believing that.

The conversation switched to lighter topics and Charlotte was feeling relaxed as she finished her poached salmon and pushed her empty plate aside.

'That was stupendous!' she proclaimed with a happy smile.

'Now are you ready for a dessert?'

'I don't know if I have room!'

'I don't know if I do either.' Jett leaned across the table. 'How about if we just have coffee here, then go home and open a bottle of my best brandy?'

Charlotte felt her stomach twist. The thought of them being alone together at the manor house was one she found immensely exciting.

She licked her suddenly dry lips and said calmly, 'OK.'

The waiter brought them each a cup of thick black espresso, and as he laid them on the table Jett asked for the bill.

Again Charlotte's stomach twisted. They'd be out of here in no time. Suddenly, her heart was beating very fast.

But, as they drank their coffees, suddenly Jett remarked, 'I believe you dropped by to see Ellen this afternoon?' he smiled approvingly. 'That was kind. How did she seem? Was she very upset?'

'She was pretty upset, but I think she'll cope. She told me her mother's coming to stay with her.' Charlotte glanced down into her cup, remembering her conversation with Ellen. 'She's very angry with Ted right now, but I think, in spite of everything, she'll stick by him. I don't think she'll walk out on him or anything like that.'

'Well, she has Lucas to think of.' Jett was draining his cup. He laid it down on the saucer with a click. 'When there's a child involved, one sometimes has to make sacrifices and accept situations one might not otherwise accept.'

'Yes, I suppose you're right.'

As Charlotte looked back at him, she was aware of a sudden fierce tightening around her heart, as

though someone had placed a clamp there and
squeezed very hard.

Was he talking about Imelda? she wondered. Had
he had second thoughts? Was he planning to stick
by the mother of his child, after all?

'No doubt about it.' He was pushing aside his
cup now. 'The plain fact is that a child brings ob-
ligations.' He paused and smiled a rueful little smile.
'That's why one should be very careful indeed about
who one ends up having a child with. Like it or
not, that person becomes a part of one's life.'

He *had* changed his mind. The clamp squeezed
tighter. Suddenly, Charlotte was finding it difficult
to breathe. Quite clearly, he now intended to stand
by Imelda and perhaps even go as far as to marry
her.

Charlotte wondered if she should feel pleased,
but feeling pleased was quite beyond her. Suddenly,
she felt desperately, achingly sick.

'Let's go.'

He was pushing back his chair and rising to his
feet, smiling at her as though nothing had altered.
Charlotte rose to her feet, too, though her legs felt
like lead.

They didn't speak much on the drive back to
Penforth Manor, but Jett seemed quite unaware of
Charlotte's sudden emotional paralysis. On the
contrary, he was humming along quite happily to
the Marvin Gaye album that was playing on the
CD.

She flicked him a nervous glance. This is terrible,
she was thinking. What am I going to do when we
get back?

And they were back, it seemed to Charlotte, in no time at all. She climbed from the car, feeling stiff and awkward, and followed Jett up the steps to the big front door. Then they were stepping inside and the door was closing behind them and suddenly they were all alone together.

'Brandy?'

Jett was leading her towards the drawing-room, but two steps from the doorway Charlotte stopped in her tracks.

'Maybe not, after all,' she said. Her voice sounded croaky. Then she just stood there, looking at him, her heart crumbling inside her.

He had turned to look at her and now he was coming towards her. 'What's the matter?' he asked, casting a frowning smile over her. Then as he came to stand before her, he reached out and touched her hair.

Charlotte felt herself freeze and melt simultaneously. 'It's—it's——' But she could not finish the sentence. And though she longed to turn and flee, she simply could not move.

Jett was watching her, those eyes like sapphires burning into her. They seemed to pluck out her heart and toss it in the air. She felt quite dizzy with the way it was spinning round and round.

Then, as she struggled against the feeling, he reached out towards her. His blue eyes smiled down at her. 'Come here,' he said.

As she felt his arms go round her, Charlotte tried to resist him. I can't, she kept telling herself. He's going to marry someone else.

But resisting was beyond her. A shudder went through her as she closed her eyes with a sigh and sank into his arms.

CHAPTER TEN

IN THAT moment, as she sank against him, all other thoughts fled. All that mattered, the only thing that Charlotte was aware of, was the incomparable, sheer uplifting magic that came with being once more in Jett's arms.

How could I ever have thought of denying myself this? she wondered.

Her arms twined round his neck as his lips sought hers, scalding her, filling her with a fierce intense longing. She sighed and pressed against him, her whole body shivering.

For there was nothing of tenderness in his kiss. It was hard and violent. It took the breath from her body. Yet she simply clung to him all the more tightly, with a kind of desperation and kissed him back with equal violence.

His hands caressed her, making her shiver, his grip on her so tight it was almost painful. And her own hands, with equal urgency, explored the hard warmth of him. For a moment they seemed locked together in a kind of desperate duel.

Then the frenzy ended and Charlotte could feel herself relax as Jett's kisses became more gentle and seductive. And suddenly she was filled with a sense of delight that burned through every nerve end and fibre of her body. Suddenly his kisses were sweet beyond imagining. As he kissed her again and again, she shivered with desire.

'Let's skip the brandy.'

Jett nuzzled against her, wrapping her in his arms as though he would never release her. He kissed her again with infinite tenderness. 'What do you say? Shall we go upstairs?'

Charlotte reached up and kissed the hollow below his cheekbone. She stroked his dark hair. 'Yes,' she said.

He swept her up into his arms then, as though she weighed nothing, and carried her up the stairs to his room in the west wing. And as they made the short journey along the corridor, Charlotte rested her head joyously against Jett's shoulder. All her earlier fears and doubts had vanished. What was about to happen felt right and natural. And it promised, too, to be the most wonderful experience of her life.

Jett shrugged off his jacket and laid Charlotte on the huge bed, bending to kiss her as he did so. He kissed her lips, her eyes, her throat, her shoulders. And between kisses, he told her,

'My lovely, lovely Charlotte. Since the moment I first met you I've wanted to make love to you. You're the sweetest, most desirable girl I've ever known.'

Charlotte reached up and lightly caught his face between her hands, and as she looked into his eyes she could barely contain the emotion that flooded through her like a torrent.

I love you, she was thinking. Why didn't I realise it sooner? I love you totally, with every fibre of my soul.

Out loud she said, 'It's what I want, too.' She kissed him softly. 'Very much.'

With a touch as light as gossamer he was stripping away her clothes, dropping her trousers, her top, her bra and her briefs, in a careless pile on the bedroom floor. And with every garment of hers, one of his was discarded, too, as with nervous, eager fingers Charlotte undid his shirt and tie, and helped pull away his trousers and belt. And though she had never been this intimate with a man before, when they finally lay naked together it felt wonderfully right.

As Jett leaned over her she could feel her nipples brush his chest, more sensitive than fingertips, making desire rush through her. Then as she gasped he caught one breast in his hand and bent to kiss it.

Whispering her name, he moulded the firm flesh in his palm, while with his finger he strummed the blood-gorged peak. Then with his tongue he began to circle where his finger had been, tightening the desire in her till it almost choked her and she could scarcely bear it any longer.

A moment later a cry broke from her throat as his lips closed around the aching, throbbing peak.

And in that moment, as her body pressed hungrily against him, she was filled with a deep sense of joy and fulfilment to think that this man, whom she loved with all her heart, was destined to become the first lover she had ever had.

With a sigh of pure happiness, she surrendered.

'You are wonderful,' Jett said. But that was a long time later, after they had made love again. And again.

Charlotte kissed his face and caressed the body she knew so well now. 'You're pretty wonderful yourself,' she said.

Jett smiled and gently wound one arm around her, so that her head nestled softly against his chest. His tone was light and happy as he told her, 'I must say I never thought I'd hear you say that.'

Charlotte laughed and kissed the dark hairs on his chest, drinking in the familiar heady scent of him. And she could hardly believe it was true as she told him, 'There was a time when I thought you were anything but wonderful. Like you said, I thought you were a bit of a monster—but that was before I knew the truth.'

Then she frowned suddenly and raised her eyes to look at him. 'There's really only one thing I still don't understand. Why were you so hard on your uncle Oscar? Why didn't you come to visit him more often?'

Jett stroked her hair softly and sighed for a moment. 'Do you really think I was hard on the old man?' he asked her.

'Not hard in the sense of unkind.' She had no reason to believe that of him. 'But maybe a little neglectful. You didn't come to see him very much.'

'No, I didn't, but it was a miracle I ever came at all.' Jett's expression had sobered. There was pain in his eyes. 'After what he did to my mother.'

The emotion in his voice made Charlotte feel guilty. She had obviously scraped against a sensitive nerve. She reached up, frowning apologetically, and kissed him. 'Forget it,' she told him. 'You don't have to talk about anything you don't want to.'

'But I want to tell you.' He smiled a gentle smile at her and drew her against him, resting her head against his shoulder. 'I want you to know why my uncle and I were never close.'

He stroked her hair again, sighed softly and began his story.

'Uncle Oscar was my mother's brother, though he was nearly twenty years older and the two of them were never close. But as I think I once told you, he was never an easy man and, as she was growing up, he was determined to control my mother's life.'

Jett sighed. 'When she decided to marry a penniless American, he was furious and tried to stop her. He cut her off financially and made it very plain to her that if she ever came back to England he would make her life a misery.

'At that point she didn't care. She was very much in love and she was more than happy to make her life in the States. But, unfortunately, my father died when I was only five and my mother never really got over it.

'Her health deteriorated, she was constantly depressed and more than anything she wanted to return to England. But she was always afraid of what Uncle Oscar would do to her, for he had never withdrawn the threats he made.

'She died fifteen years ago, an unhappy, exiled woman—and I'm afraid I never completely forgave my uncle for that.'

What a terrible, sad story. Charlotte blinked back tears of sympathy. 'How dreadful,' she told him, giving him a warm hug. 'I can't say I blame you. I wouldn't have forgiven him either!'

'I forgave him all I could.' Jett stroked her hair softly. 'In the end he regretted what he'd done. He actually asked for my forgiveness. It was partly his guilty conscience that made him leave me the house, though I told him quite frankly that I didn't want it. I would have appreciated it more if he'd been decent with my mother.'

A short silence fell. Charlotte lay quietly and watched him. So, she'd been wrong about that, too. Considering the circumstances, he'd been more than generous with his visits to Uncle Oscar.

And there was another thing as well. She'd always believed he'd been born lucky, that he was one of these people who'd just sailed through life. But that clearly wasn't so. For most of his childhood he'd had to cope with a mother who was constantly depressed. No one in their right mind could call that lucky.

She reached up and stroked his face. 'I said you were wonderful. Now I know how true that is.'

But as she looked into his eyes, through the happiness that filled her she could feel a creeping sadness lap at her heart. She was destined, very soon, to lose this wonderful man.

He was kissing her. 'I think we ought to sleep now,' he told her. As she kissed him back, he wound his arms around her. 'At least for a little while,' he added, teasing her. 'I may wake you up again in an hour or so.'

Charlotte smiled back at him, though her heart was aching. She could almost feel the sands of time trickling through her fingers. These were the last moments they would ever have together. In an hour's time, sadly, she would already be far away.

She waited, still held there softly in his arms, until she was quite sure that he was sleeping. Then she lay for a while, listening to his breathing, watching with a heart that throbbed with hopeless anguish, the outline of his profile against the white sheet.

But the time had come. Very delicately, so as not to wake him, she unwound his arm and slid from the bed. Then she was gathering up her things and sneaking on tiptoe from the room, then hurrying through the darkness to her own room in the east wing.

Less than twenty minutes later Charlotte had packed up her possessions and was loading her suitcases into the boot of her car. Then, fighting back the tears, her heart turned to stone inside her, she was driving away from Penforth Manor, knowing she must never set eyes on Jett again.

It was less than an hour and half's drive back to London. Darkness still enveloped the sleeping city and a gentle drizzle was spattering the windscreen as Charlotte drew up outside her little flat in Finsbury Park.

Home, she thought—though the thought brought her no comfort. Deep inside her heart was throbbing like an open wound.

She dragged her suitcases from the boot and climbed upstairs to her first-floor flat, then dropped the cases in the tiny hallway and went through to the bedroom.

Sleep. That was the only thing she craved now.

She flopped down on to the bed, shielding her eyes with her forearm, as though in an effort to shut out the world.

'Oh, Jett...! Oh, Jett...!' She whispered the words like a prayer. 'If only... If only things could have been different!'

As a pain like a knife went wrenching through her, she turned over with a sob and buried her face in the bedclothes. Where would she ever find the strength to live through this?

But at least you've done the right thing, she told herself over and over. You couldn't stay, not when Jett's duty is to Imelda. And surely there ought to be some comfort in knowing that?

But if there was, she couldn't find it. She could find no comfort anywhere. And as she wept into the bedclothes, overcome with helpless grief, it seemed as though nothing would ever offer her relief from the pain that tore at her poor, shattered heart.

Somewhere a bell rang, startling Charlotte from sleep. She struggled to open her eyes, not quite certain where she was, feeling dazed and bleary and shivery with cold.

And then she remembered. She was at home in her London flat. And she was lying on her bed where she'd fallen asleep after a helpless storm of weeping.

At that thought she felt her stomach turn instantly to lead. But she had no time to pause and reflect on her misery, for suddenly, shrilly, the bell was ringing again.

It was the doorbell, she realised dully. Who on earth could it be? She glanced at her watch. It was just before nine. Perhaps some friend had seen her car outside and decided to drop round.

But she was in no fit state for company, that was very clear, as she pulled herself upright and sat for a moment, frowning. Every muscle in her body ached as though beaten and the inside of her head, to say the least, felt fragile, as though someone had set about it with a kitchen scourer.

But the bell kept on ringing and somehow she had to silence it—quickly. Before her poor, battered brain simply shattered in her head.

It was an effort to lower her aching legs to the floor. But somehow she managed it and shuffled out into the hall.

'I'm coming!' she grumbled. 'I'm coming. Keep your hair on!'

Then she fumbled with the door latch and pulled the door open.

She had no time to react. Jett was in the hallway like a tornado, turning on her with eyes that blazed like blue fire.

'What the devil do you think you're doing, sneaking off like that?' he thundered. 'No note, no nothing. Is this your idea of a joke?'

Charlotte blinked at him. Her heart was turning somersaults inside her. She had thought she would never set eyes on him again, and here he was, standing right before her! The pain and the joy of it were almost unbearable.

But he had no right to be here. He was only making things harder for her. She threw him a resentful look. 'I can assure you it was not a joke. And I didn't leave a note because I had nothing to say.'

'Oh, is that so? Is that the way you do things? You make love with a man all night, then you sneak away secretly without even a word of explanation. Nice!' Jett's tone was bitter. 'A really nice way to behave!'

Charlotte had flushed at his accusation and at that reference to their night of lovemaking. 'No, that's not the way I do things,' she responded, not quite looking at him. If he but knew it, nothing even remotely similar had ever happened to her before. Last night with him had been her one and only night of love.

Her one and only and her last. The thought tore like claws inside her. But she forced herself to look at him again without flinching.

'In the circumstances, it seemed the only decent thing to do.'

'The only decent thing to do?' Jett frowned, uncomprehending. Then suddenly, impatiently, he glanced around him. 'Where's the kitchen? I'll make us some coffee. You look as though you need one as badly as I do.'

As he said it, he half smiled at her and let his eyes glance over her, taking in the dishevelled, crumpled skirt and top, her puffy, sleepy face and her uncombed hair. 'God, you look a mess,' he said.

'Thanks.' Charlotte scowled at him and dragged her fingers through her hair. 'As a matter of fact, you don't look too hot yourself.' She pointed. 'And the kitchen's over there.'

As he disappeared into it and she darted to the bathroom, to give her face a wash and tidy her hair, Charlotte reflected that it was true, he wasn't looking his best. He looked as though he'd dressed in a very great hurry, and there was a hint of a shadow around his eyes.

Maybe he was concerned about me, she thought with a flutter. It would be rather nice to think he cared that much. But more realistically, she corrected herself, rejecting the very notion, he was simply suffering from an aftermath of too much sex. Last night, after all, had been quite a marathon!

She ignored the twist in her stomach that thought instantly provoked and the sense of loss that tore at her heart. He would have nights like that again, but, alas, not with her.

When she emerged from the bathroom he had found his way to the sitting room and was laying two mugs of instant coffee on the little wooden coffee-table.

Charlotte paused in the doorway and frowned at him. 'How did you find me? I wasn't aware you knew where I lived.'

'I found out from the agency. Not today, quite a while ago. I like to know these little details about people who are staying in my house.'

Charlotte threw him a cool look. 'In case they run off with the silver? How very sensible of you to take such precautions.'

Jett did not answer her. He stood watching her for a moment. 'So, tell me, why did you run off?' he demanded. 'What did you mean when you said it was the decent thing to do?'

'Just that. It wouldn't have been right for me to stay.' Charlotte wished he would sit down. The way he was standing there, seeming to fill the whole room, made her hopelessly edgy. She glanced nervously at the little table. 'Why don't you drink your coffee?'

'If that's what you want.' He regarded her a moment longer, and she was aware again of that shadowy look about his eyes. Seating himself in one of the armchairs, he raised his mug and drank, then laid it once more on the wooden table. 'Now tell me what decency had to do with anything.'

Charlotte had known this would be hard. Wasn't that why she'd simply fled rather than confront him face to face? And she felt like fleeing again, like turning and running. But there was no point in that. He would simply come after her. She might as well just say what had to be said.

She took a deep breath, feeling her heart cold inside her. 'I was thinking about you and Imelda,' she said.

'Me and Imelda?'

'You and Imelda and the baby.'

'And what have Imelda and the baby got to do with you—with us?'

Charlotte was aware of a surge of mixed-up hope and disappointment. Was he offering her an affair, in spite of his commitments? She squashed the foolish hope—she would rather lose him than share him—and focused bleakly on the disappointment. How could she have any respect for a man who offered that?

Trembling, she drew herself up tall and looked down at him, heart beating.

'Look, you told me how you felt—that you could never abandon your child, and that for the child's sake a parent sometimes has to make sacrifices— like sticking with one's partner, even though one would rather not. And I think that's admirable.

Really, I do. But you have to realise that I have my beliefs, too.'

She took a deep breath. 'And one of my beliefs is very simple. I would never get involved with a married man. Nor with one who's about to get married.'

Jett had listened in total silence to this heartfelt outpouring, and his expression had remained still and totally unreadable. But now, as she came to the end of it, a strange thing happened. Quite inappropriately, he started to laugh.

Charlotte felt deeply shocked. Did he find her scruples amusing? Was that, after all, the sort of man he was? And that thought was so upsetting she was barely capable of taking in what he was standing up to tell her.

'You think that baby is mine? That's what this is all about?' As she stared back at him numbly, Jett took a step towards her. 'What a crazy girl you are. Imelda's baby isn't mine. How could you think such a thing? How could you think it for a moment?'

'Well, she was there at your house and you told me she used to be your girlfriend . . .' Charlotte was feeling even more stunned as his words started to sink in. She blinked at him, wondering if she dared to laugh, too. 'Is it really true, then? Is it not your baby?'

Jett had taken hold of her gently, drawing her to her feet, and he was shaking his head now as he looked down into her eyes.

'Imelda was my girlfriend once, very briefly. What we had could scarcely be described as a relationship. You see, I figured out pretty quickly that she's one of those girls who is simply out to get herself a rich husband.' He pulled a contrite face. 'That sounds harsh, I know. But from time to time one has the misfortune to meet girls like that.'

Charlotte felt a flash of understanding. Hadn't she, too, always had reservations about Imelda?

She looked into Jett's face that had suddenly grown serious again. 'So, whose baby is it?' she wanted to know. 'And what was she doing at your house?'

Jett sighed. 'After I finished with her she went off with a good friend of mine. He was unwise. He allowed himself to get quite seriously involved with her. And then suddenly she sprang this little surprise on him and started demanding that they get married.'

Charlotte was starting to understand. 'So it was your friend you were talking about?' She could feel the tightness inside her slowly slackening. 'You mean she really got pregnant deliberately, just to trap him?'

Jett nodded. 'She assured him she was taking the Pill, though now of course it transpires she was doing no such thing. Oh, yes, it was quite deliberate,' he added.

'So, why did she come to you? What did she want you to do about it?'

'She wanted me to talk to my friend into marrying her—something I wouldn't even consider doing. It was hard. She was so upset. I felt I had to be kind to her, even though I despise the way she's behaved.'

He drew a deep breath. 'I've done the best I could. My friend's offered to support the child financially, and I've managed to persuade him that he mustn't turn his back on it. He may feel like turning his back on Imelda, but he still has a duty towards the child.'

It was all falling into place. Suddenly the whole black mystery was bathed in a blessed illuminating light.

But Jett was frowning at her. 'You really believed that I was the errant father? Did you think I had no scruples at all that I would be making romantic passes at you while the mother of my child was in the same house?'

Shame-faced, Charlotte nodded. 'I made a terrible mistake.'

'Yes, you did.' He frowned at her. 'And was that why you ran away? Because you believed Imelda's child was mine?'

As she nodded again, he slipped one arm around her waist. 'So, what about last night?' His eyes looked down at her. 'Was that supposed to be your grand finale?'

A blush touched Charlotte's cheeks. 'In a way, I suppose so.' She stared at his chin. 'I wanted you so much I couldn't say no to what was possibly the only chance I'd ever have. Maybe it was wrong of me. I don't know.'

With his free hand Jett cupped her chin and gently tilted her face, so that her eyes were drawn to his.

'I'm glad,' he said. 'I'm glad you wanted me.' As she blushed, he bent to kiss the tip of her nose. 'Just how badly I wanted you is something you'll never know.'

He paused. 'In fact, I still want you badly. I want you so badly I'm going to have to make you my wife.'

Charlotte felt her heart turn over. She stared at him, speechless.

'Will you?' He kissed her again. 'Will you be my wife?'

'If you love me.' She held her breath.

Jett smiled. 'Oh, I love you. If I didn't love you I would never have made love to you last night.'

Charlotte smiled and sank against him and twined her arms around his neck. 'And I would never have made love to you either if I didn't love you.'

'So the answer is yes?'

'The answer is yes.'

Jett took a moment to look down at her and the light in his bright blue eyes was like the sun breaking through clouds after a long, dark winter. It warmed her heart and filled her soul to the brim with joy and happiness. Suddenly the future seemed vast and inviting.

Then he was sweeping her into his arms and bending to kiss her. Charlotte parted her lips eagerly. The future had begun!

SUMMER SPECIAL!

Four exciting new Romances for the price of three

Each Romance features British heroines and their encounters with dark and desirable Mediterranean men. *Plus, a free Elmlea recipe booklet inside every pack.*

So sit back and enjoy your sumptuous summer reading pack and indulge yourself with the free Elmlea recipe ideas.

Available July 1994   Price £5.70

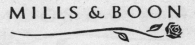

Full of Eastern Passion...

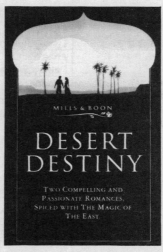

Savour the romance of the East this summer with
our two full-length compelling Romances,
wrapped together in one exciting volume.

AVAILABLE FROM 29 JULY 1994   PRICED £3.99

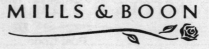

Next Month's Romances

Each month you can choose from a wide variety of romance with Mills & Boon. Below are the new titles to look out for next month, why not ask either Mills & Boon Reader Service or your Newsagent to reserve you a copy of the titles you want to buy – just tick the titles you would like and either post to Reader Service or take it to any Newsagent and ask them to order your books.

Please save me the following titles:	Please tick	✓
NO RISKS, NO PRIZES	Emma Darcy	
ANGEL OF DARKNESS	Lynne Graham	
BRITTLE BONDAGE	Anne Mather	
SENSE OF DESTINY	Patricia Wilson	
THE SUN AT MIDNIGHT	Sandra Field	
DUEL IN THE SUN	Sally Wentworth	
MYTHS OF THE MOON	Rosalie Ash	
MORE THAN LOVERS	Natalie Fox	
LEONIE'S LUCK	Emma Goldrick	
WILD INJUSTICE	Margaret Mayo	
A MAGICAL AFFAIR	Victoria Gordon	
SPANISH NIGHTS	Jennifer Taylor	
FORSAKING ALL REASON	Jenny Cartwright	
SECRET SURRENDER	Laura Martin	
SHADOWS OF YESTERDAY	Cathy Williams	
BOTH OF THEM	Rebecca Winters	

If you would like to order these books in addition to your regular subscription from Mills & Boon Reader Service please send £1.90 per title to: Mills & Boon Reader Service, Freepost, P.O. Box 236, Croydon, Surrey, CR9 9EL, quote your Subscriber No:.................................... (if applicable) and complete the name and address details below. Alternatively, these books are available from many local Newsagents including W H Smith, J Menzies, Martins and other paperback stockists from 9 September 1994.

Name:...

Address:...

....Post Code:............................

To Retailer: If you would like to stock M&B books please contact your regular book/magazine wholesaler for details.

You may be mailed with offers from other reputable companies as a result of this application.
If you would rather not take advantage of these opportunities please tick box. ☐

Win a Year's Supply of romances
ABSOLUTELY FREE!

YES! you could win a whole year's supply of
Mills & Boon romances by playing the Treasure Trail Game.
Its simple! - there are seven separate items of treasure hidden
on the island, follow the instructions for each and when you arrive at the final
square, work out their grid positions, (i.e **D4**) and fill in the grid reference boxes.

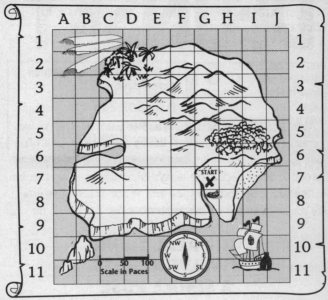

From the start, walk 250
paces to the **North**.

GRID REFERENCE

Now turn **West** and
walk 150 paces.

GRID REFERENCE

From this position walk
150 paces **South**.

GRID REFERENCE

Now take 100 paces **East**.

GRID REFERENCE

Then 100 **South**.

GRID REFERENCE

And finally 50
paces **East**.

GRID REFERENCE

Please turn over for entry details

SEND YOUR ENTRY
NOW!

The first five correct entries picked out of the bag after the closing date will each win one year's supply of Mills & Boon romances (six books every month for twelve months - worth over £90). What could be easier?

Don't forget to enter your name and address in the space below then put this page in an envelope and post it today (you don't need a stamp).

Competition closes 28th Feb '95.

TREASURE TRAIL Competition
FREEPOST
P.O. Box 236
Croydon
Surrey CR9 9EL

Are you a Reader Service subscriber?   Yes ☐   No ☐

Ms/Mrs/Miss/Mr _____ COMTT

Address _____

_____

_____

_____ Postcode _____

Signature _____

One application per household. Offer valid only in U.K. and Eire. You may be mailed with offers from other reputable companies as a result of this application. Please tick box if you would prefer not to receive such offers. ☐